Miriam's Joy!

Betty Arrigotti

BETTY ARRIGOTTI

Miriam's Joy!

BETTY ARRIGOTTI

DEDICATION

For my mother, Ruth Connor, who first introduced me to a reverence for Mary.

ACKNOWLEDGMENTS

In appreciation to all people dedicated to Our Lady. I hope you won't disapprove of my imagining Mary as joyful. Surely anyone who loves God as much as she does, must know deep happiness. So many reasons to rejoice!

I am grateful to my daughters, Theresa and Jennifer, and my husband George, who are all wonderful proofreaders and cheerleaders. And speaking of cheerleaders…

Thank you to the encouragers of the world, particularly the dear family, friends, and fans who have urged me to keep writing, even as life becomes more complicated.

My prayer is that the Spirit will touch my readers, and they will find reassurance that God is good, and that He loves them dearly.

CHAPTER 1

On a quiet residential street in Portland, Oregon, an explosion suddenly rocked the neighborhood. A fireball shot out from one house and leveled it into burning rubble. The air filled with black, acrid smoke and falling debris.

A few minutes earlier, a middle-aged woman called Miriam had been enjoying a walk in the fresh spring air and smiled when a squirrel scurried across her path on the sidewalk. She stopped to enjoy his antics, and her eyes sparkled as a second squirrel chased the first up a tree and around its trunk. The one in front spun around and a game of tag ensued, back down the tree, across the grass, and up another trunk. When a third squirrel pounced, the first two jumped in surprise and leapt to another tree, causing her to laugh aloud. Joy seemed to bubble up in the woman, and she raised her eyes briefly to the skies. She appeared to share a private joke with the clouds and then continued along her way. Suddenly she had stopped next to a minivan parked in front of a pretty two-story house, and crouched low, just before the explosion.

Inside the car that had shielded Miriam, an infant screamed. She opened the door. The last time she held a baby was centuries before car seats, but she brushed tiny cubes of glass from his lap, then deftly unbuckled and lifted the nearly bald, six-month-old boy to her chest, rocking and humming to calm his sobbing. The car seat had shielded his face and hands from the glass, and he was unharmed. Reaching a cellphone left in the front seat, she dialed 911 and reported the

1

explosion. When the baby had quieted, she climbed with him out of the car and surveyed the devastation around her.

Homes up and down the street had lost their windows. Fragments from the exploded house littered the nearest yards and street. Two trees, so recently squirrel playgrounds, now lay prone and smoldering. The house closest to her had suffered severe damage: the front half had collapsed, though the back stood whole. No other cars were parked on the street. Miriam whispered a prayer of gratitude that most of the homes were empty this time of day, with the children in school and the parents at work. But the now-only-half two-story must have housed this child's family.

"Let's go see if we can find your mama, shall we?" she crooned to the child. She walked gingerly around broken glass and scattered brick to the back of the house. When chair legs broke through a still-intact second-story window, Miriam jumped back and hunched to protect the baby from a cascade of shattered glass. A woman screamed out the window, "Help! Someone! Help us get out! I have to get to my baby in the car!"

"Look, I have your baby safely in my arms," Miriam lifted him up for her to see.

The dark-haired, brown-eyed mother looked down and some color returned to her face. "Thank God!"

"Amen. Are you all right? The front of your house is gone. Is the window the only way you can get out?"

"Yes, the bedroom door is jammed. Thank you for taking care of my Peter." She turned away. "Hush, Winnie, we'll be okay. We have help outside."

"Is Winnie hurt?"

More floor supports snapped and the house quivered. Mother and daughter both screamed, but the house paused its threatened collapse.

Miriam could hear a deep breath as the woman calmed herself. "We're both just scared, mostly, but we have to get out of here. What in the world happened?"

"The house directly across the street exploded. Use the chair legs to clear the rest of the glass from the window frame. I'm going to set Peter in the stroller I found in your car. I see a ladder next door I can prop against the window. I'll be right back."

Before long Miriam was able to lean the ladder against the house and climb up to the window. "Hello, I'm Miriam," she said.

The mother was folding a blanket over the sill. "I'm Gloria Walters. Can I hand Winnie out to you? Are you secure enough?"

"Of course."

The child, blonde but with her mother's dark eyes, began to scream again as she looked down, but Miriam quickly pulled her close with one arm. "Let's pretend I'm a fireman rescuing you."

Winnie nodded, but whimpered and clung tightly to the woman. When Miriam set her on the ground, the child looked up and said, "Hi. I'm Winnie and I'm four. Are you going to carry Mommy down, too?"

But Gloria had already backed out onto the ladder and was making her way to them. Her feet barely touched the grass before she had Winnie on her hip and ran toward the stroller to assure herself Peter was truly safe.

Miriam joined them after returning the ladder. Gloria's hand was bleeding, presumably a result of breaking the window, but otherwise, both of the rescued seemed well. Miriam pulled off the blue cotton scarf that had covered her hair and wrapped it around Gloria's hand.

"Thank you! Thank you for saving our lives." Gloria's chin began to tremble. She was at the front of the house now and could see how lucky she had been to be in the back. The whole second story on this side had collapsed, crushing all that was beneath it. "We had been in the car ready to go when Winnie said she needed to use to the bathroom. This is a safe neighborhood, so I thought I could leave Peter for that quick minute. I swear I'll never do that again!"

Miriam smiled in a way that made Gloria feel completely understood, without judgment.

"I had wanted Winnie to use the half bath by the front door, but she insisted on running upstairs."

"Judging from the look of this side of the house, that was a blessing. Do you know if any neighbors would have been home? We should see if they need help."

"No, there's only one other neighbor at home during the day, and I know she's on vacation."

"Let's get you to a clinic. You'll need a couple of stitches. Is there someone you should call?"

"I'm an army wife. My husband is overseas. We learn to manage through all sorts of things while our husbands are gone. I never thought something like this would come up, though."

Gloria's purse and phone were in the car where she left them when

Winnie needed to run back into the bathroom. Her keys were in her pocket. Once they determined the car was usable, they buckled the children and themselves into the car with Miriam offering to drive.

As they proceeded down the block, they took in the extent of the blast. For a couple of blocks each direction, windows were shattered. The houses on each side of the one that now lay flat and burning were damaged, but Gloria's had taken the brunt of the explosive force.

Gloria directed Miriam to a nearby clinic, and they parked. People crowded the waiting room, some coughing, some nearly asleep, and one or two cradling wrapped wounds. Miriam stayed with the little family and entertained several children with stories of long ago.

"My Son used to visit a cousin's farm and help with his sheep," she began telling them. "One day he was trying to catch a particularly naughty lamb. That scamp would skitter ahead of my boy just out of reach, first left, then right, then circle around behind the child, causing him to giggle so hard he had to stop and hold his sides. Just then the lamb jumped up on the backs of the flock of sheep and bounced from one ewe to another until it found its mother."

The children laughed at the mental picture she painted for them, and she laughed along with them. Her joy proved contagious and made every adult in the room grin.

With a mischievous look, she asked the children, "What is the funniest looking thing that God made on this earth?"

"Giraffes!" offered one child.

"Sea horses," said another, and the smiles began again.

"Palm trees," offered a quiet child, "they don't give a bit of shade."

"Zebras are pretty funny," one suggested. "Striped horses."

"How about these?" Miriam asked as she cupped her hands behind her ears and pushed them forward. "I think ears are hilarious." Every child in the room and a few of the adults laughed aloud. She wiggled her nose from side to side.

"Almost as funny as noses. Or big toes for that matter." She joined in the laughter, then launched softly into a song that the children all joined in whispers, "Head, shoulders, knees and toes, knees and toes…"

When it finally was Gloria's turn for the doctor to stitch her wound, Winnie clung to Miriam. Peter slept in his stroller until their mother returned, who appeared noticeably calmer.

"The doctor says the Red Cross is setting up a shelter in the local school until the neighborhood's windows at least are repaired. I think we'll need to spend the night there, while I can figure out what to do next. We sure can't sleep in our house. Miriam, where were you going when you came to my house? Do you need a place to stay?"

"I'll be fine, Gloria, but bless you for asking. I'll check at the shelter soon to see how you are doing. Goodbye, Winnie. Have fun on your adventure!"

She was out the door before Gloria could ask if she needed a ride.

Mr. Henry Martin sat by the window watching the landscape service men working, when he noticed a woman walking up the paved driveway that curved and allowed a gradual view of his large, elegant brick home. She smiled and nodded to a young man mowing the grass as she approached his porch. Henry waited for the chimes that his wife had loved and then answered the door. "Yes?"

"Hello, Mr. Martin. My name is Miriam. I'm a volunteer from the church. Someone suggested you might need temporary help. I'm very sorry about your wife."

He felt his whole body sag a bit and cleared his throat but didn't reply. The woman was of medium build with olive skin and appeared to be what people called middle-aged, older than his daughter but younger than his wife. Her outfit was simple, slacks like the ones his wife had called linen, and a loose-fitting blousy thing belted at the waist. She wore a blue scarf tied behind her neck, which made her look ready for any task. Her eyes drew his attention the most. He felt this woman could look into his soul and yet still smile at him with honest warmth. He'd seen eyes like that only once before, as a child.

The woman interrupted his thoughts. "I'd be happy to come on Tuesdays and get a week's worth of meals into your refrigerator in the morning and then work in the afternoon on any project you need done. I know you must be in a bit of a transition right now, and I'd like to help until you have decided what you want to do next."

Home cooked meals sounded very tempting. Since his daughter and her husband had returned to their home after his wife had died, he'd first gone through a month of eating whatever remained in the cabinets that didn't require work and then weeks of Italian and Chinese delivery. He couldn't imagine sitting alone at a restaurant and didn't know the first thing about cooking.

"I don't understand," he said. "Are you looking for a job?"

Miriam laughed. "No, not at all. It's just my way of giving back for all the blessings I've been given."

"I don't belong to any church. Who sent you?"

Miriam smiled, and he suddenly didn't want her to leave. He was so lonely.

"I help where I'm needed," she said.

He opened the door wider and stepped back, a bit embarrassed by the condition of the rooms. Francesca had made housekeeping seem simple. He'd never realized how much effort it took, and his energy had died when Francesca did.

Miriam stepped inside, and he followed her gaze around the marbled entry, up the curving mahogany staircase, then to the formal dining room on the left and the living room on the right. He could see she appreciated the beauty underneath the magazines and newspapers.

"Do you want to sit down and discuss this… offer?" The days had stretched so long. He would appreciate any distraction.

"If you show me to the kitchen, I can get started while we talk."

Miriam's efficient moves around the large kitchen distracted him from his embarrassment as she unloaded a full dishwasher and refilled it with the dishes that had accumulated on all surfaces. Before long the counters were empty. Ingredients she pulled out of the cupboards and the freezer soon tantalized his nose. He sat at the kitchen table and watched a graceful artist in the process of creation.

With one casserole tucked into the oven, Miriam brought over two cups of fresh coffee and sat with him at the table. He couldn't really tell where Miriam originated. She had a slight accent and her skin matched his coffee as he added milk. "What's your last name, Miriam?" he asked.

"My father called me Shapiro." She blushed a little. "It's Aramaic and can mean lovely. It can also be translated as spire in English."

"Like a church spire? Pointing up to the heavens?"

She smiled. "Tell me about your wife," she said, and his need to talk about Francesca and how much he loved and missed her filled the next hour. Somewhere in that time, Miriam had returned to cooking but gave him what felt like undivided attention while she worked.

Before long he confided in this blessed stranger about the sadness in his heart. "Francesca had always wanted me to retire early, so we could travel together. I finally did last year, though I feared I'd miss my work. We were planning a trip to tour the Holy Land when she took sick.

Jacquie Perdue slid hangers aside as she considered what to wear, though it already neared noon. Her hand lingered on her leather blazer, which she considered her reporter uniform, and she sighed. She had been off for three months now on maternity leave. She wasn't ready to return. Her heart wasn't in it. Though her heart wasn't in anything since—

She forced the thought away and closed an inner door on it. She couldn't go there. Not now. Not yet.

How did her husband do it? He had returned work as if nothing had happened. The thought of Kevin came tinged with guilt. The only emotion she could offer him lately was anger. She didn't even want to look at him; she certainly didn't want him to touch her. An involuntary shiver shook her shoulders, and she closed the closet door. Another day in pajamas. What did it matter? What did anything matter?

The phone rang, and she answered it, dropping back on the unmade bed.

Her editor at the Portland Times asked, "How are you doing, Jacquie?"

"Holding up, Sarge." She'd called him that for years, as did most of the newspaper reporters. He'd been in the military and still could pull a mean drill sergeant persona. Jacquie knew about his soft side, though, too. "You?"

"I don't want to rush you if you aren't ready, but I sure could use you back here. We've got a story I'd like to put you on. Woman's touch, you know."

She sighed. She couldn't put it off forever. Besides, she suspected this wasn't going to get easier with time. "All right. I'll be in tomorrow morning. I'm not 100%, but I'll give it a try."

"'Preciate it, Perdue. I'll owe you one."

She hung up and crawled back under the bed covers. Before long she sat up and picked up the phone. She ran her fingers through her short blonde hair while she waited for an answer. She had cut it to chin length to prepare for baby care. Now it struck her as a wasted effort.

"Hi, Dad. How're you doing?" She could talk to Henry Martin. He, too, seemed paralyzed with grief. He understood.

"Better today. You?" His voice did sound a bit lighter.

"Well, I'm here. That's about all I can say." She knew her voice sounded as heavy as ever.

"I wish we could help each other through all this, Jacqueline. Your mom wouldn't have wanted us to stay so lost."

"It's not just Mom for me, Dad."

"I know, dear. I know. It was a blessing your mother lasted long enough to hold the baby. Seems too much for one soul to handle, but you know what she would say."

Jacquie sighed. "'God doesn't give us more than we can handle.' Nice words but they don't feel true. I'm not even sure God seems true anymore."

She hadn't said it aloud before, but the distance she felt from God had been growing for quite some time. Once she moved out of her parents' home, it became harder for her to make herself go to church. She knew it saddened her mother, and when she had gotten sick, Jacquie made the effort to go more often. She begged God on her knees to heal her mom. He hadn't, and then worse yet, her sweet baby…. What kind of God would allow that?

Her father cleared his throat, at a loss as always with what to say in the face of emotions. "I had a visitor today."

Ok, he was going with changing the subject. Maybe for the best anyway. "Oh, who?"

"A lady named Miriam. She's a volunteer from one of the churches nearby. Offered to come in on Tuesdays for a while to make a few meals and do a little cleaning. Nice lady."

Jacquie's suspicions rose. "Little old lady looking for a husband?"

"No, Jacquie," he sounded exasperated. "She's middle aged and just trying to help, I think."

"You've got to be careful, Dad. Who knows what she's up to? She might rob you blind."

"Well, at least I'd get some good meals out of it." He hung up.

"Fine, be that way," Jacquie said. "I was just trying to help."

But her father's call kept bothering her. People don't just show up at your door unannounced and offer to help. Not normal people, anyway. The church should have called and asked if she could come over, given her some good references.

She mulled over the call and couldn't let go of it. Finally, she called him back.

"I'm sorry, Dad. You know I'm suspicious by nature. That helps when you're an investigative reporter," Though not in relationships, she thought. "I tell you what. Get her last name, and I'll check on her. Just humor me a bit."

He grumbled. "I know her last name. It's Shapiro. Said it's Aramaic."

"Thanks, Dad." For the first time in three weeks, something sparked her interest. Maybe she would dress, after all. She could hit the computer with a few searches.

No one would take advantage of her dad if she could do anything about it.

That evening on a television set up in the school's gymnasium, the news covered the house explosion. Gloria watched and shook her head in amazement as she once again beheld the smoldering crater that had been the house across from hers.

"Though authorities aren't saying what caused the explosion, we have just received suspicious footage from a neighbor's security camera," the newscaster said.

Gloria's eyes widened as she watched her rescuer, Miriam, crouch down alongside her car, an instant before a flash that whited out the video. When the camera recovered, she saw Miriam open the car door and emerge with her Peter.

"Police are very interested in this woman and ask anyone to contact them if they can give more information about her. She is possibly Middle Eastern, and as you saw, wears a hijab over her hair. They are not calling this an act of terrorism yet, but we will keep you informed as we learn more."

"No!" Gloria yelled at the television, and then, embarrassed she softened her voice. "She was so kind. She didn't cause this. They are jumping to conclusions, just because she wore her hair covered."

The other neighbors who had taken shelter in the gym stared at her.

"How'd she know to crouch down, right before the blast?" one of them asked. "She must have had something to do with it."

"I don't know! Maybe she dropped something. Or heard my Peter crying and bent to look in at him. I just know she's a good person. She helped me and my daughter down a ladder and out of our house. She wrapped my hand in her scarf."

"You better call the police. They are going to want to talk to you... and maybe inspect that head covering of hers."

CHAPTER 2

Gloria sat on the cot in the makeshift shelter, trying to entertain Winnie while Peter napped in a donated porta crib nearby. The echoes and vast expanse of the gym made Winnie want to shout and run, and she had trouble keeping her calm and close. She struggled to think clearly and figure out what she needed to do. She had called her insurance company and, though she didn't have any documents with her account information, they said they'd send an agent out to meet her tomorrow morning. She hadn't told her husband yet. They usually talked on a video call every second or third night during his deployment, so by tomorrow she would need to figure out how much to tell him. She didn't want him distracted when he was on assignment. He needed all his wits about him to focus on coming home safely to their little family. If only she could get her act together. How many times had she said that to herself over the years?

"Miriam!" Winnie shouted, which woke Peter, of course, who cried.

Winnie jumped into Miriam's arms, who swung her around in a circle, hugged her, and set her gently back down. "Hello, Winnie! How was your night adventure sleeping here?" Miriam patted Peter's back, and he snuggled back down into sleep.

Gloria shook her head. It had been some adventure all right. Only a few neighbors had joined her in the school gym. Most could probably afford nights in a hotel until they replaced their windows. She knew her bank account couldn't stretch for such extravagances and hoped the agent would have good news and quick money for her. She had awakened at every sound and still felt jittery.

"Hello, Gloria. How did you weather sleeping on a cot?" Miriam smiled at her in a way that made it not seem so bad after all. "I lived homeless once a long time ago. Not an experience I'd like to relive."

"Homeless." She paused. "Yes, I guess I am. But the insurance guy will meet with me tomorrow, and I'll go from there."

"Will your husband be able to come back and help soon?"

"I don't know yet. I'll talk to Daniel tomorrow night and find out. He works in Special Forces, so I don't always know when he'll be around and when he won't."

"Will you move on base?[1] I'm sure they have services available to help out."

"No, I don't think so." Gloria didn't want to go into it, but her husband didn't like living on base, and that suited her fine. He had preferred the longer commute in order to have more privacy.

"Tell me about him." Miriam settled herself next to Gloria on the cot. Winnie climbed into her lap and began to page through the picture books Miriam had brought.

"Daniel's an amazing man. I don't know how he ended up choosing me, but I couldn't have asked for a better husband."

"How did you meet?" Winnie began to suck her thumb and settled in to listen to her mom's story, but sleep claimed her almost instantly.

"Quite a knack you have with naptime," Gloria said, looking from one sleeping child to the other.

"I was 18 and trying to make it on my own. I'd been in foster care for many years by then and just wanted to be independent. I struggled more than I expected, but I was getting by. I worked as a waitress and shared a room with another girl in the same situation. Then Daniel came into the diner, and I remember feeling like I inhaled all the air in the room. He was so good looking, and his eyes drew me in like he could read my soul. Before long he started coming in almost every night, then meeting me when I got off shift, then… Well, then I went and got myself pregnant."

Miriam chuckled. "You know that's impossible, right? No woman on this earth has ever gotten herself pregnant."

"Oh, you know what I mean."

"Yes, you mean that Daniel loved you, and you loved him, and Love

---

[1] Apologies to the military. For purposes of the story, Joint Base Lewis-McChord moved 136 miles south to be near Portland.

tends to create more to love."

"I like that." She returned Miriam's twinkling-eyed smile. "Yes, Winnie came into being. At first, I thought, oh no, I made the same mistake my mom made, and I always swore I wouldn't do that. But then Daniel, who values honor above almost everything else, married me. Unlike my dad who left my mom alone to deal with more than she could handle."

"I'd say Daniel got quite a catch."

"Who me? No, he's way out of my league. I don't know why he doesn't see it, but so far he doesn't."

"I know why, Gloria. You are an amazing woman. You are obviously a very loving mother; I can tell that from how secure your children are. And so capable! Who else has their house crash around their ears and gets up and does what needs doing, even though their husband is out of the country? Who made sure Winnie escaped that upstairs room? You did. Who talked to the police and news media and told them the blast wasn't my fault? You did, thank you very much."

"Miriam, how did you know to crouch down just before the explosion? That's what everyone wants to know."

"I heard Peter fussing and bent down to see if he was all right. But wait, I was on a roll here. Who has already talked to the insurance company and convinced them to meet with you? You did."

Gloria grinned. What a funny woman, this Miriam. And yes, maybe she was right. She had managed things well, in spite of not being very educated and not very smart. Maybe, just maybe, she could feel a bit proud of herself. Maybe Daniel would, too.

Something told her Miriam would understand her fears. "I don't think I could handle living on base. The other wives, they're probably all smart and educated and know the right thing to say and do all the time."

"Why don't you think you're smart, Gloria?"

"I never was much good in school. Reading didn't come easy and everything seemed to take me twice as long as everyone else. I graduated high school, but by the skin of my teeth and thanks to some very kind teachers. I didn't come from much, family wise, you know. You could say I was what they call white t—"

"Stop!" Miriam had whispered it in order to not wake the children, but the command in her voice couldn't be ignored. "Don't say that! No one, you hear, no one is garbage. You are precious like a diamond, and so are your children. And so is your mother. She struggled with more than she knew how to handle, like you said. If men would be true *abbas*, or papas, to the children they father, families would avoid untold poverty and suffering. Mothers should not have to carry the burden of supporting a family alone." She paused, and her voice calmed. "Do you have relatives who can help you?"

Gloria shook her head, a bit stunned at the change in this woman's manner from cheery to dead serious. "I only had my mom, and she didn't stick around long. As for Daniel's family, they didn't approve of him marrying me, so he cut them off."

"Do they know about the children?"

"No."

"You'd be surprised how many parents soften when they become grandparents."

"I worry Daniel would be furious if I told them about the kids."

"Are they a danger to the children?"

"Oh no, I don't think so. It makes me sad to say, but Daniel and his parents were close until he met me. They just had higher hopes for the kind of woman he'd bring into the family."

"Well, I don't want to come between you and your husband, but your children have a right to meet their grandparents. Family is so important. Maybe Daniel would be relieved if you could broker some level of peace. And don't rule your mother out of your life forever. If, at some point you reconnect, be ready to reconcile. Forgiveness is a healing balm."

"I haven't seen her in 20 years."

"Maybe the years have been kind to her, taught her about love."

Gloria couldn't quite imagine that possibility. Wouldn't her mother have tried to find her, if that were the case?

Miriam stood and gently passed the sleeping Winnie to Gloria. "I need to leave, Gloria, but take this business card. Henry Martin is a friend of mine. If you need help, tell him Miriam sent you. He's an older man whose wife passed away recently. He has a large home with extra rooms. I suspect you could offer to do a little cooking and cleaning for him in exchange for rent until your husband is back and your life has settled down a bit. And, by the way, I seem to remember that before he became a successful businessperson, he worked as a teacher and a reading specialist."

"Where are you going, Miriam? Where do you live? I could drive you."

"I'm only visiting the area, doing some temporary work. Night shift."

Jacquie had assumed her office persona as soon as she slid on her low heels and leather blazer. Emotion was set aside, she noticed with some relief. At her desk at work, she watched the video of the woman crouching moments before a house exploded. After that she drove to the school shelter and interviewed Gloria Walters, who insisted the woman, Miriam she called her, had proven herself a good person. Maybe she was right that Miriam had crouched down near the car because she heard the child crying within. Jacquie tamped down the unexpected pain the mental image of a baby in a car seat caused her.

She decided to interview others who had met this Miriam. Strange to hear of two Miriams within 24 hours. It wasn't that common of a name, but she would pursue the other Miriam, her father's visitor, later. She drove to the clinic that treated Gloria the day before. Of course, the patients wouldn't be there, and the clinic wouldn't give her their names and addresses, but maybe the staff remembered something that would help. Too bad Gloria hadn't gotten *that* Miriam's last name.

As it turned out, three nurses had noticed Miriam, but their descriptions were frustratingly different. Well, Jacquie thought, they all agreed she handled children admirably. That had drawn their attention each time they came to the waiting room to call a patient. She had been keeping the little ones quiet and entranced with her stories and soft singing. Strangely, they all mentioned her mannerisms made them think of their grandmothers. But the agreement ended there.

Back in her car, she reviewed her notes. One described her as middle aged, fair skinned, with wavy, long brown hair. The two others thought she seemed young, maybe in her thirties, with light brown skin. Two mentioned her wearing a head covering. One called it a babushka, the other thought it looked like the veils that nuns wear. But how could she be wearing a head covering if she had wrapped Gloria's bleeding hand in her scarf? She would hardly carry spares, just in case someone needed hers!

She kept reading her notes. Medium height, medium build, according to the first and third nurse she interviewed. Slight of build and short, according to the second. It struck her that each of the women described someone who looked very much like themselves. Maybe she should count on Gloria Walter's description. She'd spent the most time with the woman. Baby Peter had distracted Jacquie while she interviewed Gloria. Sweet little guy, probably just a few months older than—

She forced the thought away and flipped back a few pages in her notebook.

Gloria described Miriam as having kind eyes. What does that even mean? Were they blue? Brown? Green? Gloria didn't remember more than that they were kind. She did say Miriam's hair was long, dark, and slightly wavy when she removed her scarf. She stood about the same height as Gloria at 5'3". She spoke with a slight accent, but not one Gloria could place. She told stories about her son when he was little, so one could assume he was an adult now, placing her perhaps in her early 40s. She proved capable of climbing a ladder and carrying a small child down safely, as well as driving. The driving didn't fit with Jacquie's image of a typical woman terrorist, if there were such a thing. Jacquie pictured them as wearing black cover-all burkas and not leaving home without a man at their side, certainly not independent enough to drive a car. That could be a misconception, though. She would check into some known terrorist women to verify.

Gloria had kept Miriam's scarf and had shown it to Jacquie. Blood stained the blue fabric, but it otherwise seemed nondescript. Perhaps there would be something a police lab could tell about it, and it surprised her they hadn't taken it when they interviewed Gloria. To Jacquie it held no new clues. So many unanswered questions. What was this Miriam's full name? Where did she come from? Where had she been headed when she arrived at the scene of the crime? Where did she go when she left Gloria at the clinic? Who was this woman?

When Jacquie finished her shift, she decided to go see her dad. In no hurry to be back to their two-bedroom condo with her husband— and the silence between them—the trip took a good 60 minutes in rush-hour traffic as she made her way to the suburbs. She parked in the driveway and let herself in.

"Hi, Dad! You home?" She looked around. The house appeared as tidy as her mom had kept it, very different than the last time she'd stopped in.

"Jacqueline, what a nice surprise." Henry Martin sat in his recliner in the living room. No television on, no paper or book in his hand. Just sitting. He stood and hugged her, then offered her the chair across from his. "What's new? How's Kevin?"

Did she really want to go there now? No, she'd tell him about the tension with Kevin another time. "He's doing okay, I guess. He's back at work. So am I, as of today." She motioned to the blazer she wore.

"That's good to hear, Jacquie. Distractions like work are good. I sometimes wish I hadn't retired."

"Mom was so happy when you did. She had big plans for you both." How cruel fate could be.

"Yes, travel. I doubt I'll do that now, without her. It was really her dream. Not mine. I looked forward to being home and spending time with…"

"Grandchildren. I know. I was so excited to share… the baby… with you." She couldn't say her name.

He reached for Jacquie's hand, but she had to wipe away escaped tears before she took his.

After an uncomfortable silence, he said, "Tell me about work. What did you do today?"

She recounted her frustrations with trying to learn more about the possible terrorist, and how varied the descriptions were.

"That reminds me of a story from my childhood," he said. "When I was little, maybe five or so, we lived in a town where immigrants of several different nationalities had settled, all surrounding one neighborhood grocery store. A one-man type of place, the owner ran it himself. He spoke with a Russian accent, and the Cold War was underway. People started being suspicious of him, and he was losing business. Then his wife fell ill, and he closed up shop to take her somewhere for treatment. People realized how convenient it had been to have that little shop nearby, and they grumbled about it not being available.

"But a couple mornings later the grocery was open, and an unfamiliar woman was at the cash register, smiling and chatting with whomever came in. The little Italian ladies swore she spoken flawless Italian, and the Austrian women were as adamant that she must be native Austrian. A few Jewish ladies said she spoke Yiddish with them. And they all said she looked like she was from their heritage. My mother sent me with a dollar to buy bread and milk, instructing me to really look at her and to come home and tell her all about the woman.

"I felt very important, like I was sent to solve a vital problem. So, I picked up the loaf of bread and a quart of milk and swaggered a bit to the cash register.

"'Good morning, Henry,' she said to me, though she didn't look at all familiar. Of course, in our neighborhood, I was used to adults whom I didn't know, knowing me. Then she smiled, and something about her made me feel all happy and loved and warm inside. I'll always remember that feeling." Henry paused a moment, then continued with the story.

"'Good morning,' I answered. 'Who are you? And where do you come from?' Nothing like a child to be direct." He chuckled.

"'I'm Mary,' she said, 'and I come from all over.'

"'Why are you here?' I asked.

"She told me then, 'The wife of the man who owns this grocery store is a good friend of mine. She knew you neighbors needed it to stay open, but he wanted to take her away for treatment for her illness, so she asked for my help. And here I am. He's a kind man, and even if people are afraid of him because of his accent, he loves his neighborhood.'

"I told my mother what she said, and she told her friends. I think they all felt a little guilty for misjudging him as an enemy. Well, they brought their business back to the little grocery store. And you know what? When they went to pay their tabs—grocery stores used to run tabs for people until payday—Mary told them that the owner had marked them all paid before he left."

"Sounds like a good man," Jacquie said, "but what does this have to do with my investigation?"

"Here's the best part. When the grocer came back—sadly after his wife passed away—he said he didn't know who the woman was. He hadn't hired anyone to replace him and didn't know any Mary who fit any of their varying descriptions. He had indeed zeroed everyone's tab, in case he didn't return, but when he checked his bank account, there was more money in it than when he left. Mary had made a daily deposit with the bank after store hours."

Jacquie raised an eyebrow. What are you saying, Dad?"

"I think my Grocery Mary might have been Mary, the mother of Jesus. I never forgot the wonderful way she made me feel. Maybe your 'terrorist' is like my Grocery Mary. Maybe she's a good woman going around helping people." He paused and dropped his voice. "Or maybe she's more."

A shiver ran up Jacquie's spine. "Dad, my terrorist's name is Miriam. What does your housekeeper Miriam look like?"

Jacquie had stayed until after dark, hoping Kevin would be asleep when she got home. Her father's description of Miriam hadn't been anything to go on, and she brushed off the uneasy feeling she'd felt when he talked about her. Instead she turned her thoughts to her marriage, or what remained of it. She and Kevin had simply coexisted for three weeks now.

She unlocked the door quietly, hoping he'd be asleep. Instead, he met her just inside the door.

"You're rocking that blazer," he said. "Back to work? That's good, I think. Isn't it? But your shift would have been over for hours. Where've you been?"

"Yes, I went back to work today, then went to see my dad. Why?"

"No reason. I'm just glad to see you up and about again."

"Yeah, it takes some of us longer to snap back than others."

"What's that supposed to mean?"

"Nothing." She moved past him and went to their bedroom to change.

He followed. "Jacquie, you know I hurt, too. Why are you keeping me at a distance? We should be helping each other through this."

She turned and looked at him. Really looked. She realized she'd been avoiding his gaze for weeks. But the love that usually rose when she studied his gentle brown eyes framed with smile lines that reached almost to his wavy brown hair, didn't resurge. Instead, pain and anger boiled in her chest.

"How can you help me through this? You did this! I don't want you to help me through. I want to be through. I want to not have to look at you. Not see you. I want you to move out." She'd said it before she really thought it through. Did she actually want him gone?

But it was too late. The words had escaped, and she could see how very much they hurt him. Well, he should hurt. He should feel every bit as much pain as she did.

"That's not fair," he said and yes, she could hear the pain in his voice. "You know it's not my fault. Nobody is to blame. It was just one of those terrible things that happens sometimes."

When she didn't answer, he turned slowly away. He pulled a suitcase from the top of the closet and tossed things into it without any logic that Jacquie could see. Her impulse was to remind him of things he would need, but she stayed silent. Then, draping some shirts and slacks still on their hangers over his arm, he lifted the suitcase with his other hand.

"You sure about this?" he asked. His eyes had lost the warmth she was used to seeing there.

She shrugged her shoulders. She couldn't answer more.

Saying, "I'll be at my dad's house, if you need me," he left, not slamming the door like she would have done, but closing it gently.

Of course, she needed him!

What had she done?

But she was too proud, too angry, and carrying too much hurt to move.

Night Shift

A priest in his fifties knelt in a chapel, long after most of his parishioners had gone to bed. A candle flickered before the monstrance that held the host, the Bread of Life, on the altar before him.

"Lord Jesus and Mother Mary, what have my brother priests done? How could they hurt the lambs we've been given to shepherd?" He began to weep. "And now I see it in the eyes of my people. They've lost their trust in priests in general and me as well. I can't lift a crying child who has fallen on the playground to my lap anymore. I can't assure a worried mother that her daughter, training to be an altar server, will be safe wherever she serves. Lord, if your people can't trust our Church, what does the future hold?"

He sobbed with grief.

Then he felt gentle, feminine hands guide his head to a soft shoulder. He startled, eyes now open wide with fear of giving scandal, but with relief saw she was an older woman, a grandmother who knew how to comfort and calm. Strange he hadn't heard her come into the chapel.

He closed his eyes and rested his weary soul. He must have slept there, against her shoulder for, what seemed like only a moment later, she was gone. A slight aroma of roses was all she left behind. He felt completely reassured and at peace, ready to continue to follow the path God set out for him.

"Bless my beloved parishioners," he whispered. "Help me shepherd them as you would."

CHAPTER 3

The next morning Miriam arrived at Henry's door carrying a bag of groceries.

"Good morning, Henry," she said, and he was suddenly a five-year-old boy again looking into the same smiling face. For the first time since his beloved wife had passed away, that familiar happily loved feeling rose and warmed his heart.

He let her in and followed her to the kitchen.

"You're her?" he asked. "My Grocery Mary?"

"Sometimes I go by Mary." She laughed in a way that made him chuckle, too.

"And, if I remember my wife's prayers right," he said, "sometimes Most Holy Virgin, Star of the Sea, Tower of David, Mystical Rose, Queen of Angels, Mother Most Pure, Queen of Families... Shall I go on?"

"No need." She was laughing again but took a small bow. "Please call me Miriam."

"It's really you? You're here visiting me? Making my coffee, right here and now? He sat at the breakfast counter and she handed him the cup of said coffee. "What am I supposed to do? Go out and tell the world? Build a church?"

She shook her head, grinning.

He almost whispered, "Why are you here? Why me?"

"Your sweet wife asked me to check on you and your daughter. I was in the neighborhood and thought I could do just that."

Henry didn't touch the coffee, but sat stunned, which made Miriam giggle again.

"So, my Francesca, she's up there?" He pointed to the ceiling. "With you and Jesus and the Saints?"

"She certainly is, and she's quite concerned for you and Jacqueline."

"She's in heaven?"

"You sound surprised." Miriam tilted her head to one side, still grinning at him.

"I am! I mean, not that she didn't deserve it, she was a wonderful woman. I guess I didn't completely believe it until this moment. I've called myself a believer all my life, but it suddenly is so much more... real!"

Miriam sipped her own coffee, perhaps to give him time to sort his thoughts.

"I should call Jacqueline, get her to come see you. You could help take away her grief." He pulled a cell phone from his pocket."

Miriam reached and touched his hand. "Not yet. Jacquie isn't ready. But I will help her, I promise."

He returned the cell phone to his pocket, but not before he considered sneaking Miriam's picture. He decided it didn't seem right.

"She was sad enough when her mama passed away," he said, "but she fell into a real dark place when..."

"When the baby died."

"Yes.... Why, Miriam? Why did that baby have to die? She was so little, and such a beautiful future awaited her."

"You know little Rosette is much happier now than she ever would have been on earth."

"I know. I guess I believe that, yes. But we're left behind, and we're devastated."

Miriam's eyes lost their sparkle. "I remember that pain. My child died, too."

"Jesus," he said.

"Children are gifts that make us better people. They're our hope for a better future. It isn't God's will to cause us pain by their deaths, but he is wonderfully capable of helping us turn our pain into blessings for others."

"I don't feel like there are any blessings in this."

Miriam nodded her head. "Grief is a terrible burden to bear. It's only possible because we know there will be a resurrection into joy."

"I miss my Francesca so badly that nothing is worth doing. I want to be with her again… even if it means dying." He allowed tears to slip down his cheeks.

Miriam reached across the breakfast bar and gently wiped them away. Matching tears rolled down her cheeks, too. "I'm sorry you hurt so deeply."

"I know I'm not the only widower grieving today. I'm probably not the only husband whose wife is watching over him. Why did you come to me?"

"Sometimes I come because the whole world needs a message, or comfort, or a reminder. Sometimes I come quietly to help one dear soul."

"I don't deserve this."

"Our Lord showers us with his gifts and graces beyond what we deserve. He wants a relationship with us, just like parents do with their children. He wants us to bring every care and thought and request and joy to Him, so He can share it with us."

"It's hard to believe He cares about one retired old man sitting alone in a recliner."

"Your wife asked me to check on you, but our Lord is the one who sent me."

Without him realizing it, Miriam had prepared and slipped two more meals into his refrigerator. She came to stand next to him and asked for his phone. He took it out of his pocket but couldn't quite believe it—though nothing seemed rational today—when she turned the phone and, smiling, took a selfie with him.

She handed him the phone, and he studied the photo. "It doesn't look like you," he said and then looked mortified by what he'd said.

"Each painting and statue is different. Maybe every photo, too." She shrugged. How do you see me?"

"Golden hair, blue eyes, amazing smile."

She looked again at the photo. "Seems today I'm a brunette with a nice suntan." She grinned. "My beauty is in the eye of each beholder, I guess."

"I like your smile. I don't remember seeing your joy depicted in art."

"How can I not feel joy when I know how much God loves me? And all my children?"

Then she became more serious. "I need to go, but I ask two things. First, don't tell people who I am, unless you want your sanity questioned or the media camping out in your driveway."

Tears had begun to trail Henry's cheeks again. He feared it would be the last time he would see her. Miriam took a tiny rose bud out of a vase of flowers he hadn't noticed. She touched the rose to his cheeks, collecting the drops of sadness. "Your tears are precious to the Lord. I will deliver these to Him."

"May I come to heaven soon, Miriam?"

She looked at him with the same tenderness his mother had when she needed to disappoint him. "Hear my second request. If someone asks you for help, treat them like you would if it were me standing before you with our Christ Child in my arms."

"I will, I promise."

"If you do that, you will have reason to live and meaning in your remaining years." He blinked, and she was gone. He wondered if he'd dreamed her visit until he found the new bounty waiting for him in the refrigerator. When he picked up his phone to look at the photo again, this time a smiling blonde, blue-eyed Miriam stood next to him.

Gloria strapped her children into their car seats and drove to her house. It felt good to have a place to go. She was thankful to the Red Cross and the school, but two cots and a porta crib sure weren't home.

She parked in front of what remained of her house. She tried to tell herself to be grateful as she considered the smoldering ruins of the house across from hers. The explosion could have leveled her house. She whispered a quiet, "Thank you, God," and started to get the children out.

A police officer came to the car. "This area is off limits, Ma'am. It isn't safe."

She boosted Peter onto her hip. "I understand, officer. That's my house. I'm meeting the insurance agent."

"You won't be able to go inside."

"No, I suppose not." Just the thought of how she'd gotten out of the house last time made her shake her head. It certainly would be nice if she could get a few things she left behind, though. Like her computer. It had been in her bedroom and probably was still fine. It would be great to get clothes for all of them.

She settled Peter into the stroller that lived in the back of the car and strapped him in, but the imagined list of possessions she would like to rescue grew. Winnie's favorite stuffed animal. The brand-new box of disposable diapers. Daniel's dress uniform with his medals. Their wedding album.

She unbuckled Winnie, who stared at their house and then buried her head in her mother's shoulder. Poor girl. How could she understand all of this when her mother didn't either?

The insurance agent arrived and introduced himself, then began taking photos. As he disappeared behind the house, an army Jeep pulled up and parked. Two more larger military vehicles followed, each filled with soldiers. A woman in the first Jeep seemed to be in charge and spoke briefly with the police officer, who took a paper from her and made a call on his phone. She walked to Gloria.

"Hello, Mrs. Walters. I'm Lieutenant Meyers. I've worked with your husband, Captain Walters."

"Did he send you here?" Had he heard about the house from someone else?

"No, Ma'am. I got a call from a woman who said she was a friend of yours. She told me about the loss of your house." She eyed the building. "And almost everything else, it seems. I'm sorry."

The police officer hung up the phone and nodded towards the lieutenant.

"We've gotten permission to remove what we can get to safely."

Gloria took a key off her keyring and tried to hand it to the woman. "We could store things in the garage until I have a place to stay."

"No need, Ma'am. I'm in charge of housing at the base, and we have a partially furnished 2-bedroom unit available for you, until your home is rebuilt."

Daniel wouldn't be happy, and until this moment she wouldn't have thought she'd ever want to live on base either, but she felt great relief to know they'd have a home, and real beds.

"I don't know how to thank you, Lieutenant Meyers."

"Thank Uncle Sam." She smiled and quietly added, "When I'm not being official, I go by Teri."

"I'm Gloria, Teri. And you are a life saver." She meant for organizing the soldiers' work to save what they could of what she owned, but also for the subtle offer of friendship.

Gloria set Winnie on the hood of her car, and they watched while the soldiers gingerly cleared away kitchen debris near the front of the house. Lieutenant Meyers stopped them suddenly and gave a command. From the back of one army truck, soldiers brought jacks that they placed to reinforce the remaining beams that supported the upstairs. Soon a parade of workers carried most of her salvageable possessions to the trucks. Under the lieutenant's orders, some things were stowed in the trunk of her car, among them the computer, clothes, and the wedding album.

The lieutenant knelt in front of Winnie, who had slid down off the car and was sitting on the neighbor's lawn, her eyes wide. "Miss Walters, is there one thing you would particularly like from your bedroom?"

"My stuffie, Spots. He's a dalmatian. I'm Winnie. And you're really nice."

"Thank you, Winnie. I'll send a search party out to find Spots. What do you think your brother would ask for, if he could talk?"

"Probably the bear blanket that he snuggles under with Mama."

"Winnie, you're a sweet sister."

Gloria beamed at Teri and would have hugged her if the woman weren't in lieutenant mode. She knew to give an officer space when in a leadership role with soldiers. For a moment she wondered how she would have responded if asked what one thing was most important to salvage for her. Then she looked from Winnie to Peter and knew she already had her treasures safe beside her. Thank heavens for Miriam!

The insurance agent returned to Gloria, clipboard in hand. "Nice to have connections," he said, nodding toward the soldiers. "I'm glad they can rescue some things for you, though I inspected a few items as they were carried past me. There's a good deal of smoke damage you'll have to deal with, and the furniture on the lower floor has glass shards embedded, so I told them not to transport it. I'll write this up as a total loss for the building, and 95% for possessions."

He wrote on his paper, then said, "Good thing you weren't home!"

"But we were."

He looked at her, incredulous.

"We were blessed to have been upstairs in my room." She pointed to it. "A 'good Samaritan' woman rescued us with a neighbor's ladder."

He looked back at the house. "It's as if some force held back the explosion in order to protect that room."

She nodded. "My son was in the car, and he was protected, too."

He walked to the car. "Where was it parked?"

"About where it is now."

He started writing again on his clipboard. "Do we carry your auto insurance, too?"

"I believe so."

He took out his camera and began taking photos of the minivan, particularly the side near the explosion. "It's amazing you could drive away."

She really hadn't seen the pockmarks and broken windows of the driver's side until she drove from the clinic to the shelter yesterday. Before that, Miriam had driven and helped Winnie into the car on that side. It had shocked her again this morning before she drove here. Her little Peter must have been so frightened before Miriam comforted him.

"Thank heavens," she said, then corrected herself. "Thank God."

On Jacquie's second day of work she scanned her computer screen, searching for a Miriam Shapiro. One hit was a death notice for an 80-year-old survivor of Auschwitz. Another was a recent birth notice. No middle-aged Miriam Shapiro had applied for a driver's license or passport, or ever been arrested. She had no car registered to her name and no deed filed for a home. Jacquie, on a whim, had even tried bat mitzvah announcements from twenty to thirty years ago. Finding no leads, she decided she couldn't devote more time to this Shapiro search. The possibility that her father's Miriam and Gloria's terrorist Miriam were one and the same seemed too unlikely.

Her editor approached her desk. "Well, Perdue, looks like I've had you on a wild goose chase. The Fire Chief just told me there was no bomb. Then I figured it was another meth lab gone bad. Crazy people think they're brilliant chemists and all they are is crazy. That stuff is so unstable it's a wonder there's any successfully made. But I was wrong there, too. Turns out it was a gas leak that blew. Lucky more people weren't home in that neighborhood. Could have been mass casualties."

"No terrorism?"

"Guess not. That lady who ducked behind the car would have died if she hadn't. Don't know how she knew, or why she ducked, but I'd say her guardian angel was working overtime that day."

"And the family across the street who lost the front half of their house had their angels, too? You don't believe in lucky coincidences, Sarge?"

"Nope, no way. Everything has a reason. I may not understand it, but I know it does."

Jacquie wished she could believe that, too. But what reason could there be for a healthy baby to die in her sleep? If there were guardian angels, why didn't the baby's angel shake her and keep her breathing? Or Jacquie's angel could have made her do something to keep her baby alive.

She sighed. Maybe God tried. She had heard the baby fuss, but Kevin had suggested they wait and see if she went back to sleep. They both had been so tired, waking every couple of hours for feedings. So, she hadn't gone to Rosette, and when the baby quieted, she assumed she had gone back to sleep. If only she had checked on her. If only Kevin hadn't told her to wait.

"Aw jeeze, what's the matter, kid? You're crying! What did I say?" Her boss wasn't any better dealing with emotion than her dad.

She sniffed, dashed the tears away with quick fingers, and shook her head to clear it. "I'm fine. Lucky family across from the blowout, whatever the reason. Sarge, I'd like to stay with the assignment. I know there's a story here."

"Whatever you want, Jacquie. Just keep me informed."

Whatever you want? She wished she'd known years before this that Sarge melted at tears. She never used to be a crier, but still, it might have come in handy.

Henry Martin opened his door to his son-in-law. "Kevin." He stepped aside. "Come in."

"Jacquie threw me out. I've been at my dad's house."

"She threw you out? What for?"

"I'm not sure, but I think she figures it's my fault Rosette died."

"The doctor said it was Sudden Infant Death Syndrome. How could SIDS be your fault?"

Kevin shrugged and hung his head. "I had suggested we move the baby to the nursery. She'd been in our room, and frankly, none of us were getting much sleep. Every time she whimpered, or sneezed, or her stomach gurgled, Jacquie and I would startle wide awake. I didn't think either of us could handle much more. I thought in another room we'd just hear her when she really needed us. We even set up a baby monitor, to be safe."

Kevin sat down in the living room and ran a hand through his hair. "You saw how tough of a time Jacquie was having. She was worried about her mom and sleep deprived on top of that. I was trying to help. I even offered to bottle feed Rosette, so Jacquie could rest.

"Then we didn't hear her when we really needed to." Kevin slumped in the chair and covered his face, which muffled his words. "Maybe it is my fault."

Henry patted his son-in-law's shoulder, wishing his wife were here. She always knew what to say.

He cleared his throat. "It wasn't your fault. It wasn't anybody's fault. Some babies don't make it." He sat opposite Kevin. "I can't believe she threw you out."

"I'm not sure she can believe it, either. She didn't say anything while I packed, but she looked shocked when I left."

Henry knew his daughter was stubborn, but she had a good heart. "What can I do to help?"

"Would you talk to her? I hate seeing her so sad. Even if she doesn't want me back, I want her to be happy again."

"I will. We have to love her through this. And pray her past it. I'm pretty sure her mother in heaven is sending some wonderful help."

"At least Jacquie is back at work. Maybe that will distract her." Kevin stood. "Thanks for listening." He cocked his head. "You seem to be happier than last time I visited."

"I'm still missing Francesca terribly, but the future doesn't seem so bleak anymore."

"I hope your daughter can turn that corner. I love her. I want to see her smile again."

"I know you do, Kevin. You're a good husband."

As Kevin left, Henry raised his eyes to the ceiling. "You hear that, Francesca? You and Miriam and I have some work to do for our daughter."

Jacquie finished her shift, but her mood hadn't lifted. She was driving home to an empty house. She'd thrown her husband—a good man, she had to admit—out of their home. Why had she done that? Why did the mere sight of him make her so angry? Could she really blame him for Rosette's death? She'd gone along with the idea of moving her tiny little one out of their room. She'd gone along with the suggestion to wait and see if she quieted when she first fussed that night. She'd been so tired, so very tired. Tired from lack of sleep. Tired of sadness. Tired of missing her mother.

When she became a mother, she needed her mom more than ever. But only weeks passed between Rosette's birth and her mother's death. After that, she kept picking up her phone to ask her mom a question about the baby, only to remember she was gone. Each time it felt as devastating as the day she died.

"God! Why do people get cancer? Why do babies die? What good is being all-powerful if you don't stop such evil!" She pounded her hands on the steering wheel, and her horn honked. People looked her way.

What was she doing driving while so emotional? She pulled over and parked to calm down. A woman approached the car and bent over to look in the window. Jacquie rolled her window down halfway, thinking the woman might need help.

"Are you okay?" the woman asked. "Oh! Jacquie!" Now the woman was beaming like they were old friends. "I'd recognize you anywhere. You look so much like your mother." The woman even clapped her hands together like a kid on Christmas.

"You knew my mom?" I don't look that much like my mother. How did she recognize me? I've never seen her before.

"Yes, Francesca and I are good friends. She's like family to me." The woman unlocked the door through the half-opened window, opened the door, and sat down next to her on the front seat.

Jacquie's suspicions rose and, though the woman was all smiles, she didn't like her taking such liberties. Red flags rose. "You are...?"

"I'm Miriam. You knew me when you were little."

Not another Miriam! Her irritation with the Miriams in the world flared. "I need you to get out of the car. I don't know you."

"Of course, Jacquie. I'm sure we'll meet again. Your mama sends her love." And then she was gone.

Not disappeared exactly. Jacquie was simply so shocked by what she had said that she must not have paid attention to her leaving. Your mama sends her love?

31

Once she was home, Jacquie called her father and told him what had happened. To her surprise, he chuckled.

"Dad!" That was not the response she expected.

"Sorry, dear. Hey, Kevin came by today."

Oh great. She could just imagine what he had to say, and she didn't want to go there. "Dad, you're changing the subject. Did Mom know a Miriam? I never heard her mention one."

"What did she look like?"

What did she look like? As a reporter, Jacquie had trained herself to notice people, to be able to describe them in detail, even if they surprised her or were only in sight for a few seconds. Normally she was very good at doing just that. But Miriam? She couldn't quite call to mind her facial features.

"She was middle aged, maybe 50, but I think pretty for her age. Fair skinned, shoulder length hair that was what? Maybe light brown?

"Doesn't sound like any Miriam I remember. Hard to say, though. Women change their hair color so easily now days." The restrained humor in his voice thoroughly irritated Jacquie.

"Dad! Did you know a Miriam? Was she a friend of Mom's?"

"Yes, dear. She was a friend, but I didn't know her at the time."

"Know Mom, or know Miriam?" Honestly, it seemed like her father was being evasive on purpose.

"I didn't know Miriam, though I'm sure I would have liked her."

"I'm not so sure. Who jumps into someone's car that doesn't know them?" She lowered her voice. "Dad, she said Mom sends her love."

"I'm sure your Mom, does, Jacqueline. I can feel her sending her love every day lately."

"Dad, she's dead!" She didn't want to be mean, but he had to face the truth. Was he losing touch with reality?

"Love never dies, Jacquie, my dear. Someone just reminded me of that. Your mother has moved on to a different life, but she will always love us both."

After a confused pause, Jacquie said, "Too many Miriams, Dad. It has to be more than a coincidence." She remembered her editor saying he didn't believe in coincidences. "What does your Miriam look like again? When will she be back? I'd like to meet her."

"Check her out, you mean?"

"Well, yes."

"I'm not sure she'll return. But I'll let you know if she does. She's blonde, by the way." He quietly added, "I think."

What did he mean by that?

"I'll show you her picture next time you come. She took a selfie with me." He hung up without saying goodbye.

She hated when he did that.

A selfie? Why would a housekeeper take a selfie with him?

In surprisingly little time Gloria had settled into the apartment. She had been busy most of the afternoon finding places for the rescued possessions. Pots and pans fared well enough, but she would need to replace dishes and everything else breakable. She would wash the clothes and the linens, for they carried the smell of smoke with them to the apartment. The children's mattresses might be a loss, too, though they served them well enough at the moment. For now, she would leave windows open whenever weather allowed. She hoped the insurance check would arrive quickly.

Three times already, though, she had answered the door to find young women with boxes of things they somehow knew she needed: baby food, cans of soup, a gallon of milk, and even a plate of sandwiches and a casserole for the next day. The ladies seemed so nice! Not sophisticated like she had feared, but down-to-earth, good women. Maybe life on base wouldn't be so bad, after all. One had said, "It's hard for all of us to be away from our original families, so we learn to build new families wherever we are stationed. We're here for you, whatever you need."

She didn't yearn for her family like they must. She never had much of a family even before she entered foster care, but she did long to be part of a group who were there for each other. Wasn't that family, after all?

Thanks to the soldiers who reassembled the youth bed and crib for her, she had tucked Peter into his crib for the night, and his bear blanket lay folded over her rocker awaiting his midnight feeding. Winnie was ready for bed, snuggling her beloved Spot. Gloria had promised she could talk to her daddy for a few minutes if she would go straight to bed afterwards and let her mommy stay to talk more.

The laptop buzzed, and her Daniel's blond-haired, blue-eyed face lit the screen and her world. She suddenly didn't know what to say. So much had changed since their last conversation.

Winnie seized the moment. "Daddy, our house fell down, but just half of it, so it's okay, and the soldiers saved Spot, and we are all in a new house. And I love you, and hurry home because I miss you, but not to our old home, to our new one."

With that she blew him a kiss, jumped off her mother's lap, and obediently headed to her new room.

Both adults were dumbstruck.

Daniel found his voice first. "Whoa."

"Yeah. Whoa."

"Please, tell me she's playing make believe."

"No, it's all pretty much how she said it. A gas leak made the house across the street explode. It's nothing but smoky cinders now. Our house took the brunt of the neighborhood damage."

She wanted to tell him how blessed they had been, but by talking aloud about it, the fear and knowledge of how close they came to death finally sank in. She wept quietly, not wanting to alarm Winnie, but it was minutes before she pulled herself back under control. It was okay now, she told herself. She could endure this with Daniel's help and not have to bear it alone. The relief of sharing the burden began to rebuild the wall of strength that had held her together.

"Aw, honey, I sure wish I could hold you right now," he said.

"I haven't been like this," she assured him. "I've been strong and capable like good army wives need to be. I don't want you to think I didn't cope."

"I know you coped; you always do. But I'm sure you must have been terrified. I'm sorry you were alone. I should have been there." His eyes told her he'd rather be with her now than on any mission.

She took a deep but shaky breath. "You weren't here, but you took care of us the same." She told him about Lieutenant Meyers and the others who came to her rescue. She told him about the wives who came to her door. "Daniel, I finally feel like we could have an extended family. That's a feeling I've never known before."

"Maybe," he said, "we shouldn't have stayed off base and kept to ourselves so much. I thought I was keeping you from feeling uncomfortable."

"You were, but maybe I need to grow up and make more connections." She wondered if now might be the moment to broach a subject she'd been thinking about since Miriam mentioned it.

She plunged ahead. "Daniel, maybe it's also time to reach out to your parents. Let them meet their grandchildren. They don't have to like me, but I bet they'll love our kids!"

Daniel scowled, and she worried she had pushed too far, but she would make one more try and then back off. "The kids might have died and never known their grandparents."

This time it was Daniel whose eyes filled with tears. He hung his head. "You're right. We never know when we'll run out of time."

Something about his voice made Gloria ask, "What happened?"

He looked at her again, maybe weighing what to say, then taking a deep breath. "Our mission was successful, but one of my soldiers didn't make it."

"Oh, Daniel, I'm so sorry. And then to hear all this from us."

"Honey, you're my touchstone. I don't know what I'd do if I couldn't look forward to this time for us to talk. Dreaming of coming back to you and the kids keeps me strong and sane. It doesn't matter about the house or our things. Wherever you and the kids are, I'll call home. But, Gloria, let me think about my folks. Don't do anything yet."

Her thoughts about family had started with Miriam, and yet she hadn't told him much about her. She now described their escape down the ladder, sprinkling it with humor to lighten the mood.

"So, when Winnie was on the ground safely, I figured I better get myself down or that middle-aged lady was going to throw me over her shoulder and carry me down the ladder next."

He did laugh, as she had hoped. She told him their new address, and though he didn't say he'd be home soon—he never could—she hoped he'd be at their new door before long.

After Jacquie's phone call to her dad about Miriam, the house felt too empty and quiet. She wandered through it and turned on all the lights. All except the nursery. She hadn't been in that room since the morning she found Rosette lifeless. She tried to push the memory away as she stood outside the nursery door, but it crashed through her defenses, unbidden. So cold. The baby had felt so cold when she grabbed her out of the crib, screaming for Kevin. They tried the infant CPR they had learned at the birthing classes, knowing they were too late. They called 911 anyway, not knowing what else to do.

Jacquie forced herself out of the memory and went to her room to change out of her blazer, slacks, and heels, and into pajamas. Kevin's pillow was gone; he must have returned while she was at work. She noticed a few more things he had taken, among them her portrait that usually sat on his dresser top. For a moment a bit of her softened. She loved him and certainly knew he loved her, too.

Her dad had mentioned Kevin came to visit him. She hadn't let him tell her more about that. Maybe she should call him back. Or call Kevin. She shook her head. She didn't have the energy. Not even to make herself something to eat. She considered climbing into the bed, but she didn't want to be there alone. Wandering back down the hallway to the nursery, Jacquie opened the door. Immediately the memories assailed her, carried by the baby-powder aroma of her daughter. It was too much. She closed the door without entering.

She returned to her room, suddenly exhausted beyond reason. She needed to lie down, to sleep. But the bed looked huge, cavernous even, and she needed cozy. She dragged the comforter off it and turned to find another place to sleep. On the way to the living room and its lumpy sofa, she stopped again outside the nursery. This time she opened the door and stepped in, desperate to be close to her baby in any way possible. Again, the aroma of baby powder. She lifted the crib mattress out of the crib and laid it on the floor. There she settled onto it, her chest nestling where Rosette had last rested, Jacquie's body curling into a fetal position, her heart growing harder and harder in an effort not to ache.

She woke in the middle of the night and walked to the kitchen. No food sounded appealing, but she poured herself a large glass of wine. When the buzz of alcohol hitting an empty stomach turned to a bit of numbness, she dragged the comforter back to her bed and sank into it. "God," she silently begged, "let me hold her one more time, even for just a minute!"

Night Shift

A man with slight greying at his temples sat on a boulder steps off a hiking trail gazing at a panorama of night sky. As the moon began to rise, he spoke aloud.

Thank you, heavenly Father, for all your gifts to us.

For the stars above us, the galaxies, and our solar system with its sun, moon, and planets.

For this earth and its beautiful oceans, mountains, forests, rivers, and waterfalls.

For our country and its dedication to freedom and justice.

For our ancestors, especially those who chose to uphold their faith and those who left their homes to make new homes here.

For our grandparents, aunts and uncles, all the people we loved who have left this life. May we see them again in heaven.

For our parents who sacrificed to give us the life we have now. Thank you for our siblings and our friends who helped make us the people we are today. Thank you for our children, who make us proud as they grow into good people. Please draw them ever closer to you.

Thank you for my spouse, my beautiful wife, one of your greatest gifts to me, who loved me as deeply as I loved her...

"What a beautiful prayer!"

The man startled at the woman's voice.

"May I sit down with you?"

He scooted to one side of the rock.

"You've chosen a lovely place to pray."

He stared straight ahead, hoping if he didn't answer she would leave him to his solitude. She didn't move or speak then, but simply regarded the starry heavens as he had been doing. Finally, he gave up. "It was my father's prayer. I used to only hear it when we were camping together. It was how he ended our conversation when we were lying in our sleeping bags under the stars."

"You were close."

"On camping trips, yes. At home we were both busy with our lives—his work, my studies—but out here was something else."

"Your mother had passed on?"

"When I was in high school. He never remarried, or even dated that I know. They were devoted to each other, and I doubt anyone else could have filled her void."

"And your father? You said it *was* his prayer."

He looked at her then, and saw a serene woman, maybe 40, with amazing compassion in her eyes. "He died today." His voice cracked, and he cleared his throat.

37

She rested her hand on his. "I'm sorry for your loss and sadness. He must have been quite a man."

"He was." He nodded slowly. "He developed Alzheimer's though, and hasn't known me for a while. Last night I visited him in his care center, and he was talking to Mom. She wasn't there, of course, but she was real to him. He was the happiest I've seen him in a long time. Then this morning he was gone. It was as if..."

"As if she'd come for him?"

He drew in a quick breath, for she had known just what he was thinking. He looked at her. "Do you think it's possible?"

"I know it is," she said. "And now they are both watching over you. They are together in the next life, and together in loving you, so proud of the man you've become and so grateful for how you took care of your father in his final years."

"I wish I could have kept him at home with me."

"He knows. And he knows you did what was best for him. Be at peace, Jonathon. All is well."

She stood and continued down the trail before he wondered about her walking without a light, and before he realized he hadn't told her his name.

CHAPTER 4

The morning arrived and awoke the awareness that stabbed the tender heart Jacquie had fought to harden. She wanted to pull the covers over her head and not move. How could she find energy to go on? But her chosen career called to her. People needed her investigations to shine light on the darker side of life. It was her job. She groaned, feeling more tired than when she'd gone to sleep, but she crawled out and stood up. She showered, and that woke her enough to don her "uniform" and the pretense that she was all right.

On the way to work, Jacquie mulled over the strange appearance of Miriams in her life. If her boss didn't believe in coincidences, how would he explain this? First the Miriam who came to "help out" her dad. Then the one feared to be a terrorist and who was, at the very least, uncannily lucky. And now the Miriam friend of her mother's, who jumped into her car. Of the three, the terrorist caught her attention at the moment, perhaps because she was in investigation mode. Then it came to her that if Miriam had an accent, but no passport, she might be in the country illegally. Though she hated racial profiling, if that bloody cloth the woman gave Gloria really was a hijab, it might be worth a second look. She wished she had asked for it, but she doubted Gloria would give it up. She seemed to cling to it like it gave her some security.

Maybe it would be unusual fabric, at least. The police lab might find DNA besides Gloria's on it. She had nothing to go on, and very little even to hold up her suspicions, but her gut told her that Miriam was not what she seemed.

Jacquie reviewed her notes from interviewing Gloria about Miriam. Explosion Miriam, she reminded herself. Even in her own mind the Miriams blended together. The three nurses all remembered her from the clinic, but all described a different woman: tall, short, slim, chunky, dark, fair. With witnesses like that, no crimes would ever be prosecuted. Jacquie remembered her father's story about the woman at the grocery store who looked different to different customers. Or at least seemed to come from their native countries. She rolled her eyes. Maybe her father was losing it.

Or maybe she was. She hadn't done much better remembering what her own Car-jumping Miriam looked like. And why, when she asked for a description of her father's Housekeeper Miriam, had he said, "She's a blonde," and then added, "I think?"

She decided to find all three Miriams and get to the bottom of this. After an hour of research at her computer, her doldrums had lifted. She was a woman with a mission. Her soul-deep sadness still threatened to break through at any time, but perhaps the search would keep it at bay.

Once her children had eaten and been dressed, Gloria gathered into a shopping bag the serving dishes the army ladies had brought to her. She buckled Peter into the stroller, and with Winnie by her side, they walked to the address of the first woman. She was ready to knock on Marline's door when the woman opened it.

"Oh!" both said.

"I was returning your plate," Gloria explained.

"Hi, Gloria. I'm afraid I'm leaving to meet some other ladies. We got word one of the husbands died yesterday, and we are going over to support his wife, Lydia. Would you like to come along?"

No, she really wouldn't, but how could she say that when they'd been so kind to her yesterday? If she remembered right, Lydia had brought the macaroni and cheese that Winnie had loved. Perhaps this Lydia was married to her Daniel's friend who was killed on their mission. She pulled herself together, mentally straightening her spine. "Of course. I'm so sorry to hear about this."

Together she and Marline walked to a small group of women, several of whom had been to Gloria's door the day before. A couple were carrying cakes. She realized she had peanut butter cookies in her bag that she could contribute. She'd made them last night after talking to her husband when she couldn't sleep. Her plan had been to give a dozen to each lady as she returned their containers. The thought gave her a boost. She could reach out to help someone else, even with as little as she now owned. Maybe she wasn't as smart as these other women, but she had something to offer.

Lydia invited them into her apartment, and each woman hugged the grieving wife. Tears filled Gloria's eyes when it was her turn. Suddenly the realization that she could lose her beloved Daniel at any time struck her as an actual possibility. She saw the same raw fear in every woman's face. Yet, courage brought them together and made this life of not knowing, of never being sure, bearable. As she poured the bags of cookies into one of the bowls that had been loaned to her, she was filled with gratitude for the strange events that brought her to this unrelated but very loving family of women.

When she visited the room where the children had congregated, she found her daughter sitting at an older girl's side, listening to stories the girl was reading. With a start, Gloria realized she had never bought books for her children, never read to them. Watching how entranced Winnie sat, she vowed to do better. Her own reading problems shouldn't disadvantage her children.

Back at home, and with both children down for a nap, Gloria smiled at the sound of a knock on her door. She had new friends! Perhaps one had come to visit.

Instead, she found the reporter Jacquie Perdue at her door. She opened it. Jacquie had been nice when they talked before at the temporary gym shelter. "Come in. I'm surprised you found me here."

"It did take a little digging."

Gloria motioned to the kitchen. "Can I get you coffee or something?"

"No thanks. I'm just here to ask a few more questions about your rescuer." She did pull out a kitchen chair and sit at the table, though, so Gloria refilled her own coffee mug, poured a second for the reporter, just in case, and joined her.

"I've told you she wasn't to blame. She was a blessing to us!"

"Yes, once they determined it was a gas explosion it removed all

41

suspicion of her, though how she knew to shield herself with the car is a mystery."

"Oh, I asked her about that. She heard my son crying and bent down to see him."

"Amazing timing."

"Yes, quite a blessing for her… and my family as well."

"Mrs. Walters, I'd really like to talk to your Miriam. Do you have any idea where I can find her?"

"I'm sorry. She hasn't said where she lives or really what she's doing here." Gloria set down her coffee mug. "Oh, she did say she's here temporarily, and working night shift. Might that help?" Gloria realized she hadn't been able to tell Miriam about her move on base, and the thought of not seeing her again brought her sadness. "If you do find her, could you give her my address? I'd love to see her again."

After finishing her workday, Jacquie once more resisted the thought of returning to her empty house. Last night's image of lying on her daughter's crib mattress embarrassed her. She decided to drive to her father's house again.

Before she was at his door, it swung open with a happy, "Jacquie, my dear. Good to see you!"

"Well, you seem chipper." Would she be able to shake off her sadness soon like him? She knew with her whole being that she wouldn't.

"Come in, come in. I just heated up one of Miriam's casseroles. Plenty for two."

"So, she's been back? I really want to meet her."

"Not since the last time we talked. In fact, I'm running out of dinners. Hope she comes again soon."

"You'll call me if she does?"

"I will. I think you two would really get along."

I doubt it, Jacquie thought, but without knowing why.

While her father lifted the dish from the oven, she laid another place setting at the kitchen table and then took a seat.

"Smells good," she admitted. "What is it?"

"No idea. Something Jewish, I suppose."

"Miriam's Jewish?"

"Originally, yes, I think so."

Again, with the suppressed humor. "Dad, what's going on? What are you not saying?" A thought made her angry. "Dad, are you infatuated with this lady?"

"No, no. Of course not." He sobered. "I'm lonely, it's true, but I still love your mother. I miss her desperately." He sat down; all happiness drained from his face. His shoulders hunched, and he cleared his throat and blew his nose, quickly wiping his eyes with the handkerchief.

Jacquie rose and wrapped him in her arms. Together they released the tears that were never far below the surface for either of them. "I'm sorry, Daddy," she rasped between ragged inhales.

He regained his composure before she did, and they shifted so he held her in his arms and rocked her back and forth.

Finally, she straightened. "I'm a mess, Daddy."

"You need your Kevin back."

She shook her head. Then she nodded. "Maybe I do need him, but I need my baby more, and that's not going to happen."

Later, when she was home again, she poured herself a glass of wine, remembering how it had relaxed her the night before. But this night she had eaten, and the effect was not the same. It took two more glasses of wine before she had calmed enough to sleep.

On the same evening, Jacquie's husband Kevin had finished his shift working on a new division of houses and, not having a home he could go to and not wanting to spend another night watching television with his dad, he stopped at a diner in their neighborhood, a place he used to frequent before he met Jacquie.

He sat at the counter and ordered a sandwich and a coffee. A man with dark hair and a trim beard and mustache took a stool next to his, which surprised him, since there were plenty of empty seats to spread out. The newcomer ordered a milk.

"Milk?" asked Kevin. "Nursing an ulcer or something?"

"No, it's simply my favorite drink. I prefer goat's milk, but cow will do. I'm Yosef," the man said, offering his hand.

"Kevin," he said while they shook. "Goat's milk, huh. Never tried it."

Yosef raised the glass the server had delivered, and they clinked their drinks.

The man was dressed oddly. It reminded Kevin of the loose woven clothes that hippies used to wear. "What do you do?"

"I'm a carpenter. You?"

Carpentering didn't fit at all with this guy's looks, but who was he to judge? "Carpenter, as well. I'm working on the new subdivision south of here. Plenty of work there if you need it. Real growth in the area lately.

"Thanks," Yosef said, and then nodded toward the sandwich that was being set in front of Kevin. "Not eating with family tonight?"

"Uh-uh." And then surprising even himself, he opened up to the stranger. "My wife is upset and threw me out. I'm giving her time to cool down."

"I'm sorry," said Yosef. "Relationships can be hard, but they are worth the work. Is she hurting?"

Now how did he know to ask that, Kevin wondered. He could have asked what I did wrong, or any number of other questions, but, "Is she hurting?"

"We both are," he admitted. "We lost our only child, our baby, to SIDS a few weeks ago." Dang it. He thought he could talk about it without moisture rising in his eyes, but he was wrong.

Yosef patted Kevin's back, resting his hand there a moment. "I'm so sorry. Nothing hurts like losing a child. And no doubt you're worried you are losing your marriage, too."

This guy was good. Kevin had to admit he'd touched on his deepest fear. Yes, he wanted children, and had loved his little Rosette, but he couldn't imagine life without Jacquie.

He could only nod.

"Give her time, but give her love, too. Ask what you can do to help. Talk if she wants to, don't if she doesn't, but find some way to serve her."

Yosef stood and set $5 on the counter. "Marriages are like a load-bearing wall. They hold up the whole structure of a family and require both supports and beams. You be her support and she'll beam." He chuckled, turned, and walked out the door.

Kevin laughed, shook his head, and then realized the depth of the man's words.

Night Shift

The rabbi's 13-year-old son joined his two new friends quietly. He had sneaked out of the house for the first time ever and was finally going to experience some of what he heard guys boast about at school. He knew the other two saw this as a joke, their worldly instruction of him, a young man carefully protected from everything that other teenagers would consider normal. The plan was to go to a party, have a few drinks, smoke some cigarettes, "or something a little stronger," the boys had said. He hoped he could meet some girls and actually talk to them without stuttering. Maybe he'd have his first kiss. "Or something a little stronger," the boys had said again, elbowing each other and laughing like they were great comedians. Then he'd be home before dawn, they assured him, and no one who knew his father would be the wiser.

But turning the corner, a woman stood right in front of them with an expression that dared them to try to pass her. She seemed ancient and leaned forward with both hands on the knob of a walking stick she had planted between them and her. She looked like she wouldn't mind using that stick on all of them.

"Reuben, is this the thanks your father gets for loving you so much?" Her voice crackled like kindling breaking in a fire.

He looked down at his shoes. What was he thinking? Everyone in this neighborhood knew him and that his father was the rabbi.

"And you, Samuel and David? What do you have to say for yourselves? What would your *Bubbe* Ruth or *Bubbe* Judith think if I should tell them what you were about to do?" Both of Reuben's friends looked panic stricken. Their Jewish grandmothers were nothing to joke about. The women loved fiercely but they disciplined fiercely, as well.

"We're sorry. Please don't tell, um…"

"You may call me Auntie Miriam. Now, go home! I'll be watching all three of you."

The boys turned and ran, each toward his own house.

Auntie Miriam chuckled and rolled her eyes. One boy turned to see if she was following them, so she shook her cane at him for good measure.

CHAPTER 5

Once she and the children were up and dressed, Gloria looked for the man's address that Miriam had given her. She would take this reading problem into her own hands, and she'd start today. One benefit of very few possessions, she realized, was not having to spend much time searching for anything. Card in hand, she buckled the children into the car and drove toward the home of Miriam's friend, Henry Martin.

A sturdy man of about 60, with grey hair and grey eyes, swung the door open with a big smile. It faltered a bit but returned. "Come in! I thought you were someone else, but what can I do for you?"

"I'm Gloria Walters, a friend of Miriam's. She gave me your address and said perhaps you could help me."

"A friend of Miriam's is a friend of mine," Henry said, then knelt down, eye level with Winnie. "Hello, my name is Henry. What's yours?"

"Winnie," she answered. "And my brother is Peter."

"Well, I am so happy to meet you, Winnie. And your brother. Please come in." He stood aside while Gloria stepped in, followed by Winnie who held tight to her mother's skirt.

He showed them into his living room and offered them seats, then said, "Excuse me, I'll be right back." When he returned, he brought a box of toys. He knelt again near Winnie and lifted a few out. "I wasn't sure what you would like to play with. Here's a doll, a magnet train, and some building blocks. You're welcome to use whatever you'd like."

Winnie sat down on the floor near the box. She began with the building blocks, then pulled the doll nearby saying to it, "You can sit here and watch me make a tower."

Gloria smiled her appreciation as Henry sat across from her. "You're good with little ones. Do you have grandchildren?"

He took a deep breath. "We just lost our first, but I hope for many more."

"I'm so sorry! I didn't mean to bring up a tender subject."

"No, not at all. Now, what can I do for you?"

"Miriam said you were a reading specialist. I was wondering if, in exchange for cooking or cleaning, you'd consider tutoring me. I can read a bit, but it seems it's much harder for me than for most. I want to read to my children and help them learn to read."

"Well that sounds like a fair exchange to me. Maybe Miriam told you I'm not doing too well in the cooking department. I tell you what, I'll teach you to read, and you teach me to cook. And in between, we can both play with your little ones in the toy room/nursery we set up when times were happier. Sound good?"

The two agreed to starting with two days a week of reading in the morning, followed by cooking during nap time in the afternoon. They began immediately. By the time the children were up from naps, Gloria had three children's books she could read fairly smoothly that she would take home for practice. Henry had mastered scrambled eggs and bacon, as well as preparing pasta with a jar of spaghetti sauce.

When Henry closed his door after watching Gloria drive away, he felt better than he had since he retired. He'd enjoyed visits from Jacquie and Miriam, of course, but by helping Gloria, he felt like his life had meaning again. He hadn't realized how deeply he missed a sense of purpose once he left work. Miriam had said, "If someone asks you for help, treat them like you would if it were me standing before you with our Christ Child in my arms. If you do that, you will have reason to live and meaning in your remaining years." He understood now, and he'd do more. He'd go looking for people he could help, rather than waiting until they asked.

Jacquie had taken her mother's address book home from her father's house the night before. When she finished her workday, she had reason to hurry home. She wanted to find Car-jumping Miriam, who had said she was a friend of her mother's. Surely, she'd at least be on the Christmas card list. But once home, she paged through the book several times and never found a Miriam. Frustrated, and not feeling like eating, she opened a new wine bottle.

The doorbell rang. She looked through the peephole. Kevin waited on her porch. "Oh God, I don't want to talk to him right now. I'm tired. I just don't have the energy."

But she figured God must not have cared, because Kevin used his key and the door opened. "Oh, sorry. I figured you weren't home," he said.

"Hi, Kev. Come in." She turned and walked back to the kitchen, realizing she was carrying the wine bottle still. "Want a drink?"

"You know I don't. I haven't eaten yet. Have you?" he asked, and she wondered if he was suggesting she shouldn't drink either. The thought made her feel defiant, so she poured a glass and drank it all in one tip.

"You okay?" he asked. "I'm worried about you. I thought you might call by now."

"Nope, not okay. Probably won't be any time soon." If ever, she thought.

He walked over and took the glass out of her hand and set it on the counter. "Jacquie, I love you. Let's not let this pull us apart."

He tried to hug her, and she went stiff in his arms. He held on anyway. Finally, slowly, she softened. Eventually she wrapped her arms around him. Then she rested her forehead against his chin. "I missed you," she admitted. The deluge of tears began again. Would they never stop?

He led her to the sofa, lay down, and opened his arms to invite her beside him. She joined him. They used to lie like this in the evenings, just snuggling together. She rested her head on his chest and listened to his heartbeat. She must have slept, because the next she was aware, he shifted, and the clock struck nine.

"Hi, sleepy head."

"That felt good. I haven't really rested well lately."

"That's because I wasn't here." He kissed her on the nose. "May I come back? I miss you."

She was afraid he'd want to go upstairs and make love, and she knew she simply couldn't yet.

"I'm sorry," she said. "I'm not ready."

She braced to counter the objection she expected, but he slid out from under her and offered to make them both some dinner before he left.

Yes, she loved this guy for a reason.

When Gloria had tucked both children into bed, she prepared her laptop for Daniel's much anticipated call. These stretches when he'd be gone, and all she had was video calls with him every second or third night, made her long for him to be home. She reminded herself she was lucky. Even a few years ago phone calls home were rare for soldiers. And her Daniel had never been gone longer than two months. But oh, how she hoped he'd be home soon. He could help her make decisions about the house reconstruction, give her time to herself without children, and keep her warm in their bed.

His call never came that night. Disappointed, she went to bed, assuring herself that it might mean he was on his way home to her. But she had seen the fear in the faces of the other military wives. She knew what it also could mean.

Night Shift

Anyone watching would have hardly noticed the two who walked that night in the grassy, tree-lined park blocks that stretched through Portland's downtown. Though a bit older than the other couples, they strolled in that way that suggests a deep love.

"I like this custom of holding hands," Miriam said quietly.

Yosef lifted their clasped hands and kissed Miriam's. "Me too." Then he drew her hand to rest it inside his bent elbow, which brought her closer, so that they were touching from elbows to shoulders. "But this is even better."

After a few more steps, she removed her hand from his elbow and wrapped it around his back. He did the same to her, laughing and adding, "Best yet."

"We never would have dared to do this at home."

"Times were different then."

"Truth, indeed. But our love wasn't less for lack of showing it publicly."

He plucked an early blooming pink camelia from a bush and slid it over her ear. "This garden reminds me of the oasis the Father brought us to on our way to Egypt."

He could see the memory shine in her eyes.

"Thank you," she said, "for your help with Kevin."

"It's my pleasure to help your many children in whatever way I can. I love you, Miriam, and I always will."

"I know, and I thank you for it. I love you, as well, and for eternity." She rested her head against his shoulder. The first time they had walked together at night had been so different, fleeing with fear for the sake of their treasured child. But after many miles, the beauty of the starlight and the warm wind of the desert had calmed them. Since then, they often enjoyed night walks together.

"Who may I help next?" he asked.

"My son Daniel. He's hurt and frightened, trying to cross a desert at night like we once did."

"I'll think of our flight into Egypt while I'm there. But I will know you are with me always."

"Our Lord is good," Miriam answered.

"Amen," Yosef replied, and the two continued their stroll, arm in arm, and deeply in love.

CHAPTER 6

In another country, Captain Daniel Walters peered across a desert at night, his rifle close to his side. He had regained consciousness in the dark, within view of the glow of his burning transport plane, but behind a ridge of sand dunes. His men had parachuted out when it was clear the plane had been hit and was going down. Being last, his chute didn't have quite enough time to fully deploy, and though he had landed in sand, he'd broken at least one ankle. He hoped the other was just sprained. He didn't know how long he'd been out—it had been dusk when the plane began to plummet—but he felt around him and realized his head had hit a rock. He might have been unconscious for hours. He forced himself to take stock of his blessings first. Thank You that I'm alive. Thank You for my helmet.

And then his mind began to cry out his fears. He quieted it with prayers.

Please let my soldiers be safe. They probably had better landings, he assured himself, since they'd jumped at a higher altitude. He owl-hooted, hoping to hear a reply. No answer.

Please let me be in friendly territory. Let me be able to walk to help. If I'm not safe, let the dark last longer and help me figure out which direction I should head.

He considered waiting until daylight, so he could look for footprints and maybe learn about where his men were or where they had headed. Waiting sounded very tempting as he gingerly stretched his feet. One could bear weight, but the other would need a splint and a crutch. He attempted to immobilize the broken ankle with a sheathed knife and his belt, then tried to lift himself upright by leaning on his rifle. It sank into the sand. He repositioned the rifle against the rock and tried again. This time he was able to stand, but the pain made him inhale sharply. He wasn't likely to be able to walk far, but the farther he was from the beacon of a burning plane, the better. Of course, if the wrong people found his footprints, they'd easily capture him.

After three steps he collapsed with the pain. It was no good. He couldn't walk. He dug a hole and buried his parachute, then used his rifle to brush away the evidence of his few steps, slung it onto his back, and began to army-crawl away from the plane. As he did, he took stock of his situation. He had grabbed a small pack as he donned the parachute. Inside would be a day's supply of water and food, a flare, and extra ammo. He placed himself in God's care and continued his sidewinding down the dune away from the plane.

Help will be looking for us, he told himself. Maybe the others have already found help. Maybe I shouldn't get too far from the plane. But a sense of urgency kept him going.

It seemed like he'd crawled for hours. It hadn't gotten any lighter, so that was good, he must not have been passed out for long. That meant if enemy forces had headed toward the plane, he had a margin of escape time. The crawling beat walking, but each swivel of his legs felt like his feet were being ripped off. He distracted himself with thoughts of Gloria and his little family. Their images kept him going after his arm muscles had long since become lead weights, and he'd spit half the desert out of his mouth and cried the other half out of his irritated eyes.

He thought about his parents. He needed to see them again. Gloria was right, they should overcome their alienation. He didn't want them to grieve over lost opportunities if he didn't make it.

He had to make it.

He began to believe that the night and the sand were both unending. Hours and miles of crawling must have passed. Going downhill he'd devised a type of roll that made good time, but uphill was nearly impossible. When he finally crested a particularly high dune, he peered over it carefully, lest he find himself rolling right into an enemy camp. At the top, two things were visible. The rising moon dimly illuminating the horizon, and a silhouette of a man with a donkey, walking straight toward him.

Forgetting himself, Daniel tried to stand to get the man's attention, but the pain shot from his ankle to his brain, jolting his heart as it passed. He dropped, unconscious.

Winnie came to her mother in her pajamas before breakfast and said, "I hear other kids playing. I want to go play, too."

It was Saturday, and all of the children who lived on base must be celebrating being out of school, because Gloria, too, had noticed the sound of happy play.

"Okay, get dressed and we'll have a quick bowl of cereal. I think I spotted a park yesterday. We'll go see what it's like." It would be good distraction for her, too, since her worry about Daniel hadn't abated.

Peter had been enjoying floor time and was even starting to scoot a bit. Before long she wouldn't be able to set him down and know he'd stay where she put him. It was a little intimidating to think about both children being mobile. Luckily Winnie was pretty reliable about coming when called. She hoped Peter would be as mellow and compliant as his sister, but if he was anything like his father, he'd be looking for adventure as soon as he was able.

Before long the threesome set out with Peter in his stroller and Winnie "helping" to push him. They followed the sounds of happy children and, within a few blocks, found the park. Gloria stopped to assess the playground for safety, but Winnie let go of the stroller and ran forward shouting, "Miriam! Miriam! I found you!"

And there, indeed, was Miriam, laughing and playing tag with some of the little ones. She turned when she heard Winnie and held out her arms to her. Winnie ran right into them, and Miriam lifted and swung her in a circle, making Winnie giggle and squeal with delight. Miriam's scarf, white and gossamer today, spun out away from its anchor like Winnie's feet before they touched back to the ground. Together they walked over to Gloria.

"Miriam! How wonderful to see you! I was afraid we wouldn't meet again when we moved here without knowing how to contact you." How could she have found them? "Did Jacquie Perdue tell you we were here? I asked her to let you know if she did see you."

"No, but when I learned you weren't at the shelter anymore, I hoped I'd find you here. Shall we walk a while?"

"I want to swing first," Winnie objected.

"Try that again, please," Gloria prompted.

"Mama, may I please swing first?"

"I did promise her some time with other children. Maybe we can sit on one of the benches after I push her a few times. Then she can play near us."

"That sounds lovely," said Miriam.

Gloria pushed Winnie while Miriam lifted Peter out of the stroller, strapped him into a baby swing, and gently pushed him. He smiled and kicked his feet, thoroughly enthralled with the experience.

When Gloria's arms were tired, she led Winnie to a nearby sandbox. Miriam lifted Peter out of his swing and, nestling him on her lap, sat next to Gloria.

"Looks like you're settling into your new neighborhood."

"I've met some nice women already." She told Miriam about the gathering for the newly bereaved friend. "Yesterday made me realize the danger my husband might be in at any time, and how easily I could be the next wife the women bring comfort to."

"Have you heard from your husband lately?"

"Last night I expected a call from him but didn't get one. That happens occasionally. His mission keeps him away from the computer." She smiled bravely, "Maybe tonight. Or he could be heading home."

Miriam took Gloria's hand and quietly said, "Dear Lord, please keep Daniel safe and bring him back home to his family soon."

Gloria blushed to hear Miriam praying aloud in public. Daniel usually quietly led their prayers at home. Yet, she appreciated Miriam's gesture and whispered, "Amen."

Peter began to fuss.

"I guess it's his naptime. He woke early today. Winnie, can you brush off the sand? We need to go home now."

Winnie frowned, then brightened with a thought. "Miriam, would you come see my new room?"

"I will, if your mother doesn't mind," she said, looking to Gloria.

"You are always welcome, Miriam. Please do come."

They walked back the few blocks to Gloria's apartment and after nursing, Peter settled down for a nap in Gloria's room. Winnie gave Miriam the grand tour of her room and introduced her to Spot, her favorite stuffed animal. "I had other stuffies, but the ones that were in our downstairs got ruined. I'm so glad Spot was upstairs. The soldiers came and rescued him."

Gloria continued the story of the other possessions they were able to extract from the wreckage of the house. "I'm pleased to have things like our wedding album and the few pieces of furniture from our bedrooms, but I realized how unimportant belongings are when it comes right down to it. I'm incredibly grateful to have both children safe."

"Thank You, Lord!" Miriam said.

"And thank you, Miriam," Gloria added.

But Miriam demurred. "I was there because He sent me there. He loves you so much, Gloria, and wants what is best for you. It won't always be easy, but He will be with you every step of the way." Miriam sighed, and then looked toward the front door.

Gloria saw two soldiers walk by her front window and heard them stop. They knocked quietly. She felt the gravity of the situation, and the gravity of her body as her legs suddenly became cement blocks and her heart dropped. She couldn't move.

Miriam opened the door for them, but then took Winnie by the hand and led her to her room, closing its door behind her.

The soldiers entered and removed their hats but continued to stand at attention.

"No," was all the Gloria could say, and she backed away from them.

"I'm sorry, Ma'am," The taller man said. "We are bringing word that the plane that your husband was returning in has gone missing. We have search parties deployed as we speak."

"Where?" Again, one word was all she could manage.

"I'm not at liberty to say, Ma'am. But please know that we are doing all we can to find them."

"Them? How many?"

"Seven souls on board, Ma'am. Four from this base, though one of them was deceased."

"Lydia's husband?"

"Yes, Ma'am. The two others are not married. You and she are our only notifications on base today."

The second soldier introduced himself as Chaplain Murphy and offered to stay with her for a while.

"Thank you," she answered, "but my friend Miriam is here. She will help."

He gave her his card and suggested that she could call him anytime and he would come. "I assure you, Mrs. Walters, the army will do everything they can to bring them home."

Alive, she prayed. Please God bring him back alive.

As they turned to leave, a thought came to Gloria. "Wait! Will you notify his parents?"

The younger soldier answered, "We have no contact information for them, Ma'am. If you can give me their address or phone number, I'd be honored to do that."

"No, no. I think I should. But thank you."

They left, and Miriam came out of Winnie's room and hugged Gloria until she had stopped shaking.

When she had calmed, Gloria asked, "What do I do now? The thought of Daniel marrying me so upset his parents that they wouldn't come to the wedding. Now I'll be the bearer of bad news, but I couldn't let them go through what I just did, seeing two soldiers in dress uniforms at their door."

"Perhaps," said Miriam, "the grandchildren can ease the way."

Gloria nodded. She hoped the contact information for Mr. and Mrs. Walters had been rescued from the other house. If it were anywhere, it must be in Daniel's desk. The soldiers had carried it full down the creaking stairs and brought it to the apartment. She had never looked in its drawers. Never needed to, before now.

When she found their five-year-old wedding invitation, unopened and marked, "return to sender," she ignored the hurt his parents had caused and instead focused on being grateful that Daniel had kept it. "I've got it!" she told Miriam.

"Will you go see them?"

"They live in Eugene, only a couple hours away. I could go tomorrow after church and arrive by early afternoon. If I had found a phone number, I could let them know I'm coming, but maybe in this case, showing up on their doorstep with two little ones will keep them from turning me away. And if they do, well, I tried. If it were my son, I'd want to know."

"Do you need money?"

"Daniel always insisted on having a small emergency fund. I think even he would call this an emergency, don't you?"

"I do."

"When I talked to him about trying to mend fences with his folks, he asked me to wait until he had thought about it a while and was home."

"But now?"

"Well, now I have to make a decision without him. That's what military spouses have to do sometimes." Gloria was surprised to realize how edifying her own words were.

She could do this. Then if Daniel came back—when Daniel comes back, she corrected herself—he might come back to a healed family. The image of her being part of an extended family was the dream she needed. She could risk the chance of their rejection of her, if there were any chance of her children knowing loving grandparents.

As a child she had once torn the cover off an old magazine and taped it to her wall. It was a Norman Rockwell illustration of a happy family crowded around a Thanksgiving table, giant turkey and all. Everything in her yearned to be part of something like that. And if she couldn't, well, she'd do everything possible so her children could.

Dear God, please let their daddy be part of that dream, too.

Jacquie woke midmorning Saturday, remembered that Kevin had spent the evening with her, and turned to be sure it hadn't been a dream. A bit disappointed to see his side of the bed empty, she recalled how he'd left before bedtime with a little kiss on her cheek. No objections, no arguments, just a kiss, a whispered, "I'm here to support you in whatever you need," and he was gone. That was nice, she told herself and almost wished he'd stayed.

She stretched and sat up. Saturday. How would she fill her day without work, a husband, or…? Her thoughts wouldn't obey her and turned to Rosette. Her arms yearned to hold that sweet child. She wanted to smell the top of her head and nuzzle against her cheek.

She thought of the nursery, with the crib mattress still on the floor. She was relieved Kevin hadn't seen that. She got up long enough to use the bathroom, drop the mattress back into the crib, and then stumble back to bed, her grief and the short time in the nursery more than she could endure. She wished she had thought to bring the wine bottle to bed. Maybe she could find the buzz that took the edge off the pain. Even that wasn't worth getting out of bed for, though.

In the middle of the afternoon, Kevin called. She ignored her phone and went back to sleep. When hunger woke her after dark, she used the bathroom, found the wine bottle, and returned to bed.

Night Shift

A young, frightened teen couldn't believe it. Until tonight, she had hidden her pregnancy for almost nine months. Luckily, she wasn't like those slim, blonde cheerleaders who would have shown within the first weeks. She had donned baggy sweats once she realized what was happening, and no one had guessed. Not many really looked at her, anyway. But then, tonight, her mother must have noticed, or maybe she finally saw how her "stepdad" ogled her. Before she knew quite what was happening, her mom had thrown her out of the house. Well good. She'd never have to avoid her mother's boyfriend and his roving... everything... again. But where would she go right now? She had no close friends to ask for help. No teachers who made her feel seen, let alone special.

She had walked about a mile in the dark—the Portland's spring rain feeling colder than usual—simply wandering, trying to figure out where to go. Suddenly she felt her first, but terrifyingly strong contraction, and with that, her water broke. "Oh God! Oh God! Jesus, Mary, Joseph! Help me!"

It wasn't supposed to happen this fast. She'd read about deliveries in the school library. She figured it would take hours, but instinct told her she would give birth in a matter of minutes. Her back had been aching all day; could that have been the beginning? She scanned her surroundings, realizing that she couldn't make it far in this condition. She wasn't in the best part of town, the rows of apartments around her were in the same disrepair as the one her mother rented, but then she spotted shelter beneath some stairs that led up from the sidewalk to a building's front door. It gave her enough seclusion and cover that she might remain hidden, if only she could stay quiet. She slipped into the dark, bumping into a bicycle locked and stored there. If this baby came without anyone else knowing, maybe she could take it somewhere safe, leave it, and go back to her normal life.

Another contraction nearly laid her flat. She squatted and panted like in the movies she'd seen. She gritted her teeth and allowed only a whispered, "God, help me!" to escape.

Who was she kidding? Her life would never be normal again, and she could never go back to her mother and the creep she let live with them. She felt hopeless.

Suddenly she realized she wasn't alone under the stairs. Of course not, she thought, houseless people know all these makeshift shelters. However, another contraction kept her from being able to move.

"Shh, don't be afraid. You're going to be all right," a woman's voice whispered. "I'll help you."

Who was she to argue? She'd asked God for help. Maybe this was His doing.

The woman took off her coat and motioned for the girl to remove her pants. She covered the girls' naked legs with the coat, tenting it over her raised knees. From the little light that made its way to them, the woman seemed surprisingly clean, considering she probably lived under these stairs.

"Thank you, ma'am," the teen offered between pains.

"I'm Miriam. And you?" She stroked the girl's forehead, calming her.

"Shasta." Dang, she shouldn't have used her real name. This all had to be done without anyone knowing who she was. But the lady radiated calm and smiled so nicely. Maybe she could be trusted. Another rising pain cut off any other thought.

"You're doing fine, Shasta. Your little one is in quite a hurry. I see the head already. You can push with the next pain."

As if she had any choice! Though her body was young, it knew exactly what to do, and push she did! She thought her teeth might break with the effort of clenching back the screams that seemed to rise from her deepest insides and demand release.

Another push and she felt the child slide out between her legs. Such relief she'd never known!

"A little girl, Shasta, and she's beautiful! Just like you!"

No one had ever called her beautiful before, but she set that thought aside and reached for the now crying child. Her child. Her own.

Miriam cut the cord, then swaddled the baby in her headscarf, and handed her to Shasta. Her little daughter quieted immediately, as if she knew her mother. After she managed one more contraction and push, Miriam wrapped the placenta in something Shasta couldn't see. Miriam cleaned her gently and lovingly, which brought tears to Shasta's eyes. She felt completely loved by this stranger.

Giving the baby to Miriam to hold, Shasta pulled her pants back on.

Taking her little one back, she wrapped her in Miriam's coat to keep her warm. She stroked the child's cheek and gazed into her dark eyes. The baby seemed to look back at her with complete trust. How could she leave this little one anywhere? She couldn't even bear to have her out of her sight.

"What am I going to do?" Shasta asked.

"Your grandma has been praying for you. I think we could go to her."

Shasta didn't think to ask how Miriam would know this. Such things seemed minor on a night of miracles like tonight. She wondered aloud about it later, though, once she had been safely welcomed into her grandmother's home. Her grandma simply smiled, as if she knew a secret.

CHAPTER 7

Gloria hurried to get her children ready for the drive. She packed a lunch with plenty of liquids. Nursing, she was always thirsty now, but at least she wouldn't need to worry about bottles for Peter. Entertaining him in his car seat would be another matter. She hoped Winnie would help with that. Figuring she'd begin to drive when it was time for Peter's first nap, she stopped at the chaplain's Sunday morning service. Afterwards, she gave him her cell phone number, in case he learned more about Daniel's whereabouts, and hopefully, his rescue. The other wives that she had met came to her with words of encouragement, but she could see that same fear in their eyes. A fear she now knew personally and might never overcome again.

She drove an hour before Peter woke. Both she and Winnie needed a rest stop. After they'd used the bathroom and changed Peter, Gloria pulled Winnie's little trike out of the back of the minivan and encouraged her to ride and get her wiggles out. She spread a blanket on the grass so that Peter could stretch a little and then laid out a simple picnic. She wanted Winnie to see this as an adventure and didn't let on just how frightened she was, both about Daniel being missing and meeting his disapproving parents for the first time.

After another hour of driving, she followed her phone's directions to the street where Daniel had grown up. She prayed they hadn't moved and were home. She prayed for wisdom in choosing her words. She prayed for courage. After parking in the driveway of a modest but trim ranch style home, she slipped quietly out of the car in order to not awaken two sleeping children. She knocked on their door hoping she could talk to Daniel's parents on the doorstep without Winnie hearing, but still be able to keep an eye on the car.

To the right of the house, she heard a crash and then a groan. She ran to see if someone needed help.

Around the corner of the house a ladder had tipped sideways, taking a balding man in his late 50s with it. He swore softly and rose to his hands and knees before looking at her. "Who are you?"

"Are you okay? Can I help you up?" All Gloria's rehearsed introductions eluded her. "Mr. Walters?"

"Yes." He did not look friendly, though his features matched many of her beloved husband's. "I was cleaning gutters. I leaned too far over to see who was in our driveway." He waved away her attempt to help him up and stood, towering over her by several inches.

"I'm Gloria, your son's wife." She again offered her hand, this time to shake.

His eyes widened, and he turned away, brushing dirt off his hands and pants instead. "Figures," he said, then looked toward the front door. "Margo, you better come here."

A woman with hair the color of Daniel's joined him, drying her hands on a dishtowel. "What happened? I heard a knock at the door, but no one was there." She looked at Gloria, clearly waiting for an explanation, but then noticed the ladder on its side. "Are you hurt, Pete?"

"I'm fine. Hip and shoulder will give me trouble tomorrow, no doubt. This is Daniel's wife, uh…"

"I'm Gloria. Nice to finally meet you." She wished she hadn't said, "Finally," but it was too late to take it back.

The woman's lips tightened. She studied Gloria, as if she was an insect that was creepy but fascinating. "What do you want?" Margo asked, none too kindly. "Money? That's not going to happen. We made that clear to Daniel."

The sound of her husband's name and her worry about him straightened her back and reinforced her resolve. "I'm not asking for anything," Gloria answered, and she heard the shortness in her voice. This was not going well. But what did she expect? They'd never extended any type of acceptance before, and she'd shown up on their doorstep, or on their lawn, unannounced.

"Mama, I need to go potty," an insistent voice from the car yelled.

Gloria looked at the car and sighed.

"Quick, Mama!"

"I guess I do need to ask to use your restroom." But when she looked back at her in-laws, their demeanor had changed.

"We have a grandchild?" They both now wore small, lopsided smiles.

"Two," she answered. She hurried to the car and released Winnie from her seat. The child bounced out of the car and hurried to her grandmother.

"Hi, I'm Winnie. May I use your potty, please?" she asked as politely as any mother could wish.

While Gloria unbuckled Peter, she caught a glimpse of Margo, with a dreamy expression on her face, taking Winnie's hand and then leading her into the house.

"And who is this little man?" a much softer-voiced Mr. Walters asked as she again approached the house.

"This is Peter. He's six months old." She waved his little hand and watched his grandpa melt.

"Peter. My namesake." The man who had seemed so rigid a moment before, now reached out. "May I hold him?"

Gloria followed her children and their grandparents into their home, all too aware that the news she carried would ruin the magic she had witnessed.

When Jacquie awoke, her head felt like someone had used it as a bowling ball. She rolled over, and the motion made her catapult to the bathroom. She didn't quite make it in time and had to clean up what little had been in her stomach. The smell made her retch again, but now only dry heaves remained. She hadn't felt this particular kind of sick since college. She dropped back into bed but heard her phone buzz with a text message. It was from her boss.

"There's a Captain Walters missing. Friend of mine on base just called. Might be the owner of the house that lost its front half. Go see what you can learn. You've interviewed his wife, if I'm right."

A second buzz.

"Sorry about calling you out on Sunday."

Jacquie groaned. She wasn't fit for work. She sure wasn't fit for driving. Knowing she was risking Sarge's disapproval and maybe even her job, she didn't answer. Let him assume she was in church.

But lying there, she began to think about Gloria. What a horrible thing to happen, right after losing her home. No doubt she agonized over what this might mean. That brave lady had handled the explosion admirably, but to lose a husband, too? And with tiny ones depending on her?

Jacquie's stomach churned with guilt. She had thrown her husband out. A good man who loved her. She'd walled herself off from him. Gloria's loss made her realize how lucky she was, and how very selfish she was being.

When the room had stopped spinning, she made herself some coffee, dressed, and arranged an Uber to take her to the army base.

The day didn't go well. On the base, there was no answer at Gloria's door. A woman approached her, asking if she could help. She confirmed it was Gloria's husband who was missing but didn't know where Gloria was or when she'd return. The chaplain had been a bit more helpful, though her pounding head had kept her from really focusing on what he said. She left knowing Gloria had gone to talk to her husband's parents, but not who or where they were. Gloria hadn't answered her phone.

Sarge wouldn't be at all happy with her lack of progress on the story. But the temptation to numb the desperate need for her daughter made her scribble a note to leave at Gloria's door and order another Uber ride to take her home. Once there, she discovered she had finished the last of any alcohol in her house the night before. "Just as well," she muttered, and taking two extra strength pain relievers, she crawled back into her unmade bed.

The evening brought Gloria back to her apartment on the base. No new word had arrived about Daniel, but she wouldn't lose hope. She trusted his unit to spare no effort in finding him. She hoped, and also prayed, he would be alive and return home safely. After she tucked her children into bed, she reviewed her day and felt good about her decision to see Daniel's parents. Daniel's mother had served them all an early-afternoon snack, and then Winnie had fallen asleep on the couch watching a cartoon while Peter napped in his grandfather's arms. With both children asleep, Gloria told her in-laws about the reason for her visit, and as expected, they were heartsick at her news. They rallied around her though, promising to make the trip to the base soon to be with her until the ordeal was over. She had left after their talk, with the children tucked into their car seats, hopefully to resume their naps on the way home. But before she backed out of the driveway, both Daniel's parents had hugged her and thanked her for reaching out and apologized for their earlier behavior. She had been four years old the last time a parent had hugged her. The feeling warmed and calmed her throughout her drive home.

She knew not to expect a call from Daniel, but she still was disappointed when the usual call time came and went. God willing, she consoled herself, Daniel would survive and come home soon. She prayed he would be as pleased by the reconciliation as his parents were.

Night Shift

A nun knelt in prayer in front of a seat in the hospital chapel. Her spirit felt broken and she hoped for some healing in this sacred place. She tried to reach out to God, to beg Him for reassurance, but she couldn't reach that elusive place of peace where He sometimes met her. Eyes closed, she sensed someone kneel next to her. Strange she hadn't heard anyone enter the chapel.

She opened one eye to steal a peek. A woman about her age was deep in prayer with such serenity that it made Sister Jerome feel like an imposter. The woman turned toward her. Her eyes were strikingly gentle. "You've lost someone you love," the woman said, and her empathy felt as warm as a physical embrace.

"Yes, my best friend, Sister Andrea."

"I'm so sorry for your pain."

"Thank you, um…?"

"Miriam."

The nun eased back onto the chair behind her and Miriam did, too.

"Miriam, I know I should be happy for her. She's in heaven, I'm sure. Our ultimate reward. The ending that makes this life meaningful. But all I can think is how much I'm going to miss her."

"You'll be lonely." The woman's words were less question than acknowledgement.

"I will. And my life will change drastically now. You see, Sister

Andrea and I were the last two sisters in our convent. I'll need to return to the mother house now, which isn't a bad place, but this convent has been my home for more than 30 years."

"What was Sister Andrea like?" Miriam asked.

"Loving. Patient. As a young woman, I'd been denied by three other convents and was near to giving up on my vocation when I visited her convent." Sister Jerome chuckled in spite of the quiet of the chapel and the burden in her heart. "You see, I'm a bit of a clown. I love an audience and can entertain one for as long as they'll let me. Whether it's a parade of jokes, one after another, or a line from a movie that fits the occasion perfectly, I love to make people laugh. When I played little pranks on the other nuns, Sister Andrea would just raise her eyes to heaven, like she was praying for patience. Nothing hurtful mind you, just helping us all take ourselves less seriously." She shook her head, remembering lighthearted times.

"She loved you just the way you are," Miriam said. "My Son is good at that, too. But those non-judgmental souls leave a vacuum when they're gone. A hole in our joy."

"You're right, absolutely right." Sister Jerome looked at the woman. She might be a nun herself. Her clothes were simple, a blouse and skirt. Her pale blue scarf or veil wasn't familiar, though, so not from a local convent. Yet, she seemed familiar, somehow. "Have we met?" she asked.

"Not in person, though I've been a fan of yours for years," the woman answered. "I'm sad about you losing your home."

Sister Jerome looked at the serene woman intently, still feeling she was missing or forgetting something. Finally, she shrugged. "We simply haven't attracted new young women for far too long. Some convents are having a resurgence, but not ours, I'm afraid."

"It's too bad, Sister, that you haven't ever been sent to speak at local Catholic high schools. Joy like yours is contagious and might have brought in new girls. Maybe you could visit, tell them about life in a convent. I bet from your perspective it can be a hoot!" Then she winked and added, "It's never too late to spread the faith."

Sister Jerome gasped. Miriam had quoted Sister Andrea's final words. "Did you hear her say that to me?"

Miriam simply bounced her eyebrows, exactly how Sister Jerome would after delivering a punchline. Her words touched the nun's soul, raising tears that blurred her vision. When she blinked them away,

Miriam had gone.

Days later, after Sister Andrea's funeral, a letter arrived while Sister Jerome was packing for the mother house. It seemed her Mother Superior had come up with "an inspired idea" to send her on a trip across the country, visiting Catholic high schools and colleges to encourage new vocations. The coincidence made her shiver, then laugh, then do a little victory dance, and then silently thank God for Miriam, wherever and whomever she was.

CHAPTER 8

Half a world away, and nighttime again in the desert, Lieutenant Daniel Walters woke to find himself watched by a man and a donkey. The man, dressed in light Bedouin-type robes and holding a long walking stick, put his finger to his lips in warning. The moon gave enough light to see that the man drew a simple fish in the sand with his stick. He smiled at Daniel, then motioned for him to drink what turned out to be milk. Not cow's milk, but some kind of milk. It was thick and probably nourishing, so he drank deeply, but the pain had unsettled his stomach, and the milk didn't feel like it would stay down.

Realizing he might be trusting this man too quickly, he reached to reassure himself that his rifle remained slung over his shoulder. It wasn't, and fear made him lurch away. The man held both hands out as if to calm him, then pointed at the rifle, tied to the donkey. He motioned again, and though Daniel realized he wanted him to mount the donkey, he couldn't quite fathom the little burro carrying his large body. The nomad motioned again, so Daniel tried to hoist himself upright. The pain from his ankles assured him he could not walk, and the man's furtive gesturing made him realize they could not stay where they were. He rose to his knees and pulled himself astride the donkey, the sheer agony of the motion causing him to vomit. The little beast was so short that Daniel's toes dragged the ground. The man took a rope from the donkey's back and wrapped it around the donkey's chest and Daniel's shins so that his knees were bent, and feet were no longer dangling. The rope was tight enough that his ankles didn't move, but

68

not so tight he would worry about circulation. With his ankles immobilized, the jostling of the willing little animal was just bearable.

The man led the animal between dunes for what seemed like hours. Judging from the North Star, Daniel figured they were travelling northeast. It didn't help him much, since he didn't know which direction he had army-crawled the night before, or even quite where the plane had crashed. But finally, the horizon began to lighten and the donkey, whose ears had been flattened against its neck, now raised them. It seemed a strange thing to notice, but in the dark, and surrounded by nothing but sand dunes, the donkey's ears were about all that Daniel could make out. That and the back of the man who was leading him, somewhere.

As the sun began to clear the horizon, his rescuer turned with a broad smile. "You're safe now."

They crested one last hill and Daniel looked down at an oasis. Tall palm trees reached for the sky, grass covered the ground, and a young boy was releasing sheep from an enclosure. The sheep followed him as he called to them and walked towards a hillside.

"I hope you are Daniel Walters," the man said.

"I am." Daniel reached out his hand and they shook. "And who is my rescuer?"

"I'm called Yosef."

"And you're a Christian? That's what the fish you drew meant?" He remembered that from Sunday school.

Yosef chuckled. "I've just always wanted to do that. I was born a Hebrew, of David's line to be specific, but became a follower of Jesus. The fish drawing was used years after that, however."

Daniel couldn't figure out what he meant, but Yosef was untying his legs, and his feet dropped painfully when the rope released them. He gasped but didn't cry out.

"How did you know we were safe?" Daniel asked after Yosef had eased him gently off the donkey. "You announced it before the oasis was in sight."

"An oasis can be a beautiful destination, or a refreshing place to rest. My wife is my oasis." Then he answered Daniel's question. "I watch my friend's ears." He pointed to the donkey, who was nibbling at grass nearby. "He doesn't like angry men and seems to sense when they are around and keeps his ears down. When they go up, I know we are among friends. Good thing you weren't an angry man."

Yosef offered him another drink, saying, "Best goat's milk around. I've missed that."

His rescuer sat near him and brought out a hunk of cheese and a knife from a bag around his waist. He sliced some for Daniel, and then ate some himself. Next, nuts were produced and shared. Daniel wished he had saved something from his own small pack to offer, but he'd emptied it during his long army crawl before Yosef found him.

"Thank you, Yosef. You certainly saved my life. How did you find me? And why care for me so generously? I wish I had something to give to thank you. Wait, I have some cash in my wallet!" He began to fumble to pull it out, but Yosef stopped him.

"I have all I need. My Son taught me to care for those in need, even you Samaritans." He laughed.

Daniel was confused. "Americans? You mean Americans?"

"Samaritans, Americans," he shrugged. "Anyone in need is my neighbor."

"But did you just happen upon me? When I first saw you in the moonlight, it was like you headed straight for me and knew right where I was. And how did you know my name?"

"Miriam sent me."

He says that as if it explains everything, Daniel thought.

"She said you need to get back to your wife and two little ones." Then he looked quite pointedly at Daniel. "And reconcile with your parents."

How did he know about his wife and children? Who was Miriam? The name seemed familiar. Hadn't Gloria mentioned a Miriam? And his parents. Yes, he needed to return to his parents. But first he desperately needed to sleep.

Jacquie woke at 3:00 a.m. with a start. She had been dreaming of a car accident, one that she'd been the first driver to come across a couple of years ago, and which had occasionally haunted her with nightmares ever since. She sat up in bed and turned on the light to dispel the images of blood and bone and broken glass. She shivered, not from cold but from memories.

Teenagers had been drinking, she'd learned from the police report, and she'd processed her horror of the experience by writing an article about the senseless loss of life. She'd sworn to herself never to drink and drive, not even after one single beer, knowing that the ability to decide whether one was impaired was the first bit of reason that alcohol attacked.

Her own recent drinking haunted her now, and she tossed restlessly in bed until she admitted to herself that she had to get herself under control. She wanted to rebuild her life, do her job well, and recover, if at all possible, from the death of her mother and her child. Overindulging would prevent all that.

When she awoke again a few hours later, she felt more clear-headed than she had in a while. She checked her phone, but there was no response from Gloria. Feeling a surge of energy, she changed into fresh clothes, made her bed, tidied the room, and started a load of laundry.

Thinking more about her story assignments, she sat down at her computer with toast and coffee to begin a short article.

Dear Readers,

This writer has been following leads about an unusual woman who has performed acts of kindness for people around our town. If you have been helped by someone named Miriam, a stranger to you, please email me and tell me your story. Include a description of Miriam and any other information you learned about her.

When she had emailed the brief notice off to the paper, she sent her boss another short article that summarized the little she had learned about Gloria's husband. Feeling less than adequate as a journalist, she made up for it the rest of the day setting her house back into order.

When the kitchen, living room, and her bedroom felt sufficiently clean, Jacquie stopped outside the nursery door. Was it time? Could she go in and survive the emptiness? The emotional boost she had built by cleaning the other rooms spurred her on. She opened the door, steeling herself against the aroma of baby powder. No, it was too much for her. She slammed the door closed. After a deep breath, hand still on the doorknob, she opened it just a little. She inhaled, let herself adjust to the scent of the room and then entered. The crib mattress still lay crookedly in the crib from when she had slept on it. She felt embarrassed that, if she really had needed to sleep in the room, she hadn't thought to use the rocker recliner they'd bought for night feedings. That night, however, she had needed to lay her face where her Rosette had slept.

Squaring her shoulders, Jacquie lifted the mattress, removed the sheet, and carried the mattress to the closet. Next, she dismantled the crib and carried its pieces to the closet. Picking up the sheet, she imagined inhaling deeply of its aroma, but instead tossed it into the hamper which still held a few of Rosette's sleepers. Stifling the sob that threatened to rise, she carried the hamper and after moving a load to the dryer, dumped its contents into the washing machine. She added detergent and started the load but stopped it immediately. She snatched out a sleeper that hadn't gotten wet yet and held it close to her cheek. It smelled of stale urine, so she dropped it back into the machine and restarted it. She could have returned to the nursery to box and store the baby clothes there, but she decided she had done enough in that room for one day. Instead, she went to the garage, removed the infant seat from her car and stored it in the nursery closet. This time, before leaving the room, she opened a window a few inches and left the door wide open to air out the room. Maybe that would blow away any lingering guilt, she thought.

She gathered every empty alcohol bottle and can, surprised and shamed by how many containers there were. In the morning she would carry the bin out for the recycling truck to pick up. She'd put an end to this self-pity drinking.

By nightfall she felt pleased with herself and found she was ready to sleep without the aid of a nightcap. Perhaps she had discovered a better way to keep her pain at bay, by staying busy.

Night Shift

An elderly man sat in his kitchen chair, opposite an empty chair, drawing it close as if sitting knee to knee with someone.

"Hi, Mary," he said quietly. "Almost bedtime and it's our chance to chat. Please come pray with me and make my humble thoughts worthy of your Son."

He took time to fully imagine Mary sitting with him in her white dress, her hair covered with a blue mantle but peeking out a bit on her forehead. He imagined her eyes glowing with love for him, and the image reminded him of the women who had loved him in his life: his grandmother, his mother, two sisters, and his sweet wife. They were all gone now, but he looked forward to seeing them again when he passed on.

Since losing his wife several years ago, he had begun praying like this each evening. Talking to a woman like he used to with his wife soothed his loneliness. He was still praying to God, but with Mary, his own prayer partner.

"Thank You, Lord, for the beautiful morning. You know I can't walk as far as I used to, but I still made it around the block and I thank You for that, too. Your trees were pretty with the little green buds and even a few plum blossoms."

He continued. "I thank You for the phone call from my son today. I know he's busy, and I suspect You give him a nudge now and then to give me a call. Thank you for the years that have passed and the memories they provided me. I am sorry I wasn't a better parent, but I trust You can take up where I left off and heal any wounds that I caused my children. You know I always tried to do right by them."

He sat up a bit straighter, stretching his back, and hearing his joints creak. His body wasn't anything like the strong, muscular man he used to be, but he had come to accept that over time.

"I thank you for my daughter. I sure enjoyed her stopping by with her grandkids. That little one sparkles. Takes after her great-grandma, God rest her soul."

His mind wandered as he remembered the youngest singing for him and doing a little dance. He started worrying about the children's future, but as soon as he realized it, he focused back on the chair opposite him.

It was no longer empty.

"Mary!" he gasped. "Is that you?" He looked around him. Everything else was still the same. He didn't think he was dreaming.

"It is, Pat. I enjoy our nightly talks so much that I thought I'd come tell you that tonight."

He blinked his eyes several times, but she still seemed to truly be there, just as he had always pictured her.

"You came here, just for me? Why me? I'm nothing special. I've made so many mistakes."

"Pat, you are tremendously special to me and to our Lord, as well. We are delighted with your gentle faith. You've loved well and lived well, touching more lives for the better than you could possibly realize."

He felt awe-struck and tried to sink to his knees, but with a gentle hand to his shoulder Miriam stopped him. "Rest, Pat. You're tired."

And he was. Deeply. All the way to the marrow in his bones. The effort to hold his head up became more than he could manage.

"Come home with me, Pat. Many loved ones wait to welcome you."

"But my family here—"

"You'll still be with them. They'll know you by faith now, instead of seeing you, but they won't forget you. The two-way love will continue, even more rich than before. Love never ends."

The health monitor he wore alerted the agency that he had fallen. When he did not respond to their questions, they called an ambulance and his daughter. She arrived first and the smile and peace on his face comforted her. "Mother Mary came," were his last words to her.

He surely had not suffered and had not been alone.

CHAPTER 9

Daniel woke and found himself lying in a small cave that smelled of animals and wet wool. He didn't remember anything since overlooking the oasis.

"Welcome back to the land of the living," Yosef said, and offered him another drink of the goat's milk.

What he really wanted was a strong cup of coffee and some bacon and eggs, but he wasn't in a position to be choosy. "Thank you," Daniel said, "for taking care of me. Where are we now?"

"Still near the oasis. I walked there earlier in order to get you some bread. I thought you needed a good rest, though, before the next leg of your journey."

"Not our journey? You aren't coming along?" He looked out and figured it was at least midday. "How long was I asleep?"

"A full night, and half of today. You were exhausted." He broke another large piece of bread off a flat loaf, spread something on it and handed it to Daniel. "You should be very hungry."

Daniel nodded, realizing the truth of the observation, but he worried about how long he'd been missing, and what Gloria must be going through, if she knew.

"I need to get home. Can you help me?" But he'd no sooner said the words than he heard the unmistakable sounds of a helicopter.

Yosef grinned and motioned outside the cave. "Your journey continues." He walked to the mouth of the cave, waved his arms while looking up toward the sky, and then returned.

"I don't know how to thank you, Yosef. I'll never forget you."

Yosef shook Daniel's hand with both hands and held his gaze. "Go love your family, carrying peace in your heart. Go with God."

A phone call woke Gloria in what was still the small hours of morning in the States.

"We have him, Mrs. Walters! He's safely in the air and headed to a location where he will be evaluated medically."

Gloria could feel the rise of the adrenaline in her system that the phone ringing had caused. "He's safe? He's alive?" She had to be sure she had heard the message right and not dreamed or hoped herself into a false belief.

"I'm told he may have two broken ankles, but according to Captain Walters, he was well cared for by a man named Yosef who led him on a donkey out of danger." The voice on the other end of the phone chuckled. "He might be a little disoriented."

She took offense that the man cast doubt on her husband's words. "Was he far from the crash site?"

"Quite far, Ma'am. Upwards of 30 miles."

"And he certainly didn't walk that far on two broken ankles."

"No, Ma'am. I guess he didn't."

She felt bad then for challenging this herald of good news. "I apologize. Let me start over. Thank you for letting me know. And for all that was done to get him to safety. This is wonderful! When will he be home?" Usually she wouldn't have asked about when an assignment might end, but she felt a right to know this time, when he obviously could no longer be involved in any special operation.

"I can't say yet, Ma'am. It will depend on his medical evaluation, but I doubt it will be long. Good night, Mrs. Walters. I hope you can get back to sleep."

"I'm sorry, I didn't catch your name."

"I'm afraid I didn't introduce myself in my excitement. This is Chaplain Murphy."

Gloria felt even worse. She'd admonished a chaplain. "Good night, Chaplain Murphy. Thank you again for the welcome news. God bless you, Chaplain."

"And you, Ma'am, and Captain Walters as well."

"Amen," she said, without really thinking. But hanging up the phone, she sank back under the covers, feeling she could exhale for the first time in days. Her thoughts rose to heaven with deep, deep gratitude.

Once it was a reasonable hour, she called her newfound parents-in-law, Margo and Pete. They decided they would drive to the base to welcome their son whenever he arrived, and to make peace.

Next Gloria returned the reporter Jacquie's call and shared her good news.

When a sleepy Winnie came out of her bedroom, Gloria picked her up and hugged her tight. "Daddy will be coming home soon!"

Winnie giggled and Peter stirred in his crib. Gloria realized how very much—in spite of houses exploding and the dangerous work her husband did—she had to be grateful for.

Jacquie reviewed the notes she had taken during Gloria's call. She felt great empathy for this poor woman who had lost her home and could have lost her husband in the same week. She thought of Kevin and how she might have felt if it had been him missing and in danger of being dead. And yet, he was missing, she realized, and she'd been the one to send him away. Suddenly she yearned to see him, to know he was safe and not a world apart.

She dialed his cell number.

"Hello?" He sounded a bit irritated. Glancing at the clock she realized he would be at work. "Jacquie, is everything okay?"

Her first reaction was to be defensive, but she took a calming breath before she spoke. "Kevin, I miss you. I'm so very sorry for throwing you out. Will you come home? Come back to me?"

She heard a muffled, "Yes!" and imagined him grinning and pumping his fist. In fact, she could hear the smile in his voice when he answered, "I'll bring pizza so that we don't have to cook. See you after work!" Then he lowered his voice, "I love you, Jacquie!"

"I love you, too, Kev. I'm glad you're safe."

"I won't be if my boss sees me on the phone. Back to work, dear. See you tonight."

The phone disconnected, and Jacquie stretched her back and rolled her shoulders. Tension melted away from her muscles. Grief and heartache were still her companions, but maybe with Kevin she could face them in a healthier way.

She checked her laptop and heard several pings as email downloaded. Her request for stories about Miriam had run this morning, and already she had numerous answers. Each one became a new lead for tracking down this mysterious woman. Or women.

It occurred to her that maybe there was a group of generous women who did kind works and all called themselves Miriam in order to remain anonymous. That had to be it! That would explain the varied descriptions of Miriam that filled her emails: fair, dark, middle aged, young, with the writers guessing by her accent that she was Latina, Irish, Middle Eastern, and one that swore she must come from the same village in Kenya that the writer had emigrated from.

Gloria spent the morning preparing for the arrival of Daniel's parents, hoping they and he would be together soon. She peeled her sheets off her bed, deciding to give her bedroom to her guests. For now, she could share a bed with Winnie in the second bedroom. For a brief moment she wished she were welcoming them into the little house that she had loved, but she straightened her shoulders and reminded herself to be grateful for what she had. She knew Miriam had set the wheels in motion for the army to salvage what they could from her house, and then to find her a new home on base.

The thought of Miriam made her wonder where her rescuer had gone and if she would see her again. That reminded her of Henry, and she realized she was almost late for her biweekly reading lesson and his cooking lesson. Throwing the sheets into the washer was a delay, but one that was necessary if her in-laws were to sleep on clean bedding when they came. She only had the one set for her bed. She called Henry to apologize that she would be a few minutes late, then hurried the children into the car. Winnie didn't complain. She enjoyed the attention Henry always gave her.

As Gloria settled Winnie in the adjoining room, now stocked with new toys, and buckled Peter into a carrier on her chest, Henry placed a simple reader on the kitchen table and poured her a cup of tea. He had made great strides in housekeeping, Gloria noted, though his cooking skills were rudimentary at best. As was her reading, she reminded herself.

"Did your parents read to you when you were little?" Henry asked.

As usual, questions about her childhood made Gloria freeze. What to say? She didn't want sympathy, but there wasn't much she could say that wouldn't evoke it. She struggled, and he waited patiently.

"No, I don't remember being read to," she finally answered. It was sad, but simple answers usually were enough to help the moment move on and the conversation take a new turn. This time, though, it didn't work.

"Why in heaven's name, not?" Henry shook his head in disbelief. "Every parent should know how important it is to read to their children. Not only to help them develop a love for reading, but also to open new worlds to them."

She shrugged, but he was undeterred. "What about Dr. Seuss? His books are delightful in how they play with our language and introduce poetry. One Fish, Two Fish, Red Fish, Blue Fish?"

She shook her head.

"Little House on the Prairie? Wrinkle in Time? Children can experience limitless adventures along with the characters in such books!" He sat down, looking almost defeated.

"That's why I need to learn to read better," she said quietly, "for Winnie and Peter not to miss out on such things."

He sighed deeply. "On that note, let's begin," he said, and she could hear the compassion and patience in his voice.

When her lesson had ended, she set Peter down on a blanket on the floor near Winnie. They moved to the kitchen counter where she became the teacher and he the student. Today she would show him the basics for a variety of casseroles. Her confidence returned during this part of their visit, and she realized how brilliant Miriam had been to allow them both to retain their dignity by trading their knowledge.

"Have you seen Miriam lately" Gloria asked.

"Not for a few days," Henry answered with a sigh.

"She certainly brings joy with her, doesn't she?" Gloria set a cutting board in front of Henry and demonstrated the safe way to chop carrots. He took the knife from her and began his new task slowly and carefully.

"But when she leaves, and you can't help but notice a sense of..." He looked at Gloria, searching for the right word.

"Loss?"

"Yes! Loss. Like she took more light away than she brought with her. But then you start looking for ways to bring the joy back, and it makes you try new things and look for people to share her joy with."

"That's true! I went looking for Daniel's parents! She was part of that decision." Gloria told Henry then of Daniel's disappearance and the relief she felt learning he was safe. "But there was a blessing in it, I think. Now I've met his parents, and I think we can grow closer."

"Miriam has inspired me, too. I've been reaching out more, looking for people I can help. That's brought me such pleasure. I signed up to be a Big Brother, and I'm considering going to the local school to be a reading aide. We'll see how I do with you first."

"Well, you've certainly helped me. I'm grateful to Miriam that she introduced us, or rather, sent me to you."

Henry nodded, and then gently prodded. "Gloria, why weren't you read to? What happened?"

Gloria sat back down at the table and drew her teacup close to her, taking a slow drink before she began. She hadn't told her story to anyone but Daniel before. She leaned to check on the children through the kitchen doorway. Her daughter was happily helping two sock puppets talk to each other, telling their own simple stories.

"My dad left before I was born. I don't know anything about him, even his name. My mom struggled on her own, but I don't think we were ever stable. At least, I don't remember any sense of safety. Looking back as an adult, I think Mom was bipolar. She'd be all energy and fun, throwing caution to the wind, and then she'd turn dark and slow and pretty much stay in bed." She could have stopped there. That would have been enough to tell him, but she imagined Miriam nodding to go on, and the image compelled her forward.

"When she was down, I was often hungry. One day when I was four, I decided to make something to eat. I was tired of the cereal or peanut butter and jelly sandwiches I almost lived on, so I took out a can of spaghetti from the cupboard. I was so excited. I was going to surprise my mom and make us both a hot dinner." She exhaled as if to release some of the pain the memory brought.

"I did pretty well. I managed to open the can without cutting myself. I turned on the gas flame under one of the stove burners and poured the spaghetti out into the pan above the flame. I was using a dishtowel to keep from burning my hand on the pan handle." She looked at Henry but was only seeing her four-year-old self the moment her life had all gone wrong.

"The dishcloth must have touched the gas flame. It was suddenly on fire. It burned my hand. I screamed and dropped it on the floor. My mom came rushing from her bedroom and stomped out the fire. She ran my hand under cold water. She was both hugging me and yelling at me, and the cold water hurt my hand."

She could have stopped there. That was enough to have admitted, but the momentum of the story made her continue.

"She put me to bed. I was afraid to come out of my room, and it still makes me sad to think I never got to eat that spaghetti. The next morning, she woke me and held me on her lap rocking me for a long time. I thought she had forgiven me, but then she told me she was going to take me to the hospital for the doctor to look at my hand. She wrapped a white cloth around it, and we walked to the car. Once we were near the hospital, she told me to get out and walk in while she parked the car. I did." She swallowed, but her voice cracked anyway. "I never saw her again."

Henry place his hand over hers, over the one she had burned twenty years ago, and she realized tears were rolling down her cheeks.

"So, you went into foster care? Were you adopted?"

"After what seemed like forever someone noticed me in the waiting room. They called the police and children's services. No one ever found my mother, that I know of. I didn't know her name. She was just Mom. And I didn't know my own last name. I guess she'd never thought to teach me that. Winnie is the age I was then, and she certainly knows so much more than I did."

"Winnie is very bright, and I bet most of that is because of you. Your mother should have taught you more."

Gloria shrugged. "I went into the system. I never was adopted, maybe because they couldn't end my mother's rights without finding her, or maybe it was something about me."

"I'm sure you weren't to blame. You're a lovely person." Henry certainly looked sincere, though Gloria didn't believe him.

"Have you looked for her?" he asked. "Would you want to? I could help, if you'd like."

Gloria considered his offer. For so long, finding her mother would have been a dream come true. Now as an adult, maybe she should just be grateful for her husband and her children.

If only she hadn't tried to make the spaghetti. Maybe her mother wouldn't have hated her.

Did she still?

"Thank you, Henry. Let me think about that." It was all she was ready to decide.

Yosef settled into a chair at the diner counter next to Kevin and ordered a lemonade.

"Really? Lemonade? I figured you for a goat's milk man," Kevin said.

Yosef looked at him, laughed and they shook hands. "Hello, Kevin, nice to see you again. I've been out in the desert, and I've discovered there is nothing as refreshing when you are dry than lemonade. It even beats goat's milk."

Kevin shook his head and laughed. Yosef was an odd duck, but he found himself liking him all the same.

"And you?" Yosef said, motioning to Kevin's empty cup. "What can I buy you?"

"I'm a coffee man, myself, but I'll try a lemonade. Thanks."

"Last time we talked, you were procrastinating heading to your father's house. Still not back at your own home?"

"I actually was invited back tonight, and I was really hyped. I even bought flowers and pizza, but then I drove up and parked. My wife had put the recycling out—usually my job—and the bin contained the biggest collection of empty alcohol bottles I've ever seen at our house. I don't drink, and Jacquie, my wife, usually only has a glass of wine here and there."

Yosef looked at him, not seeming to understand.

"It was disgusting. She must have been on quite a binge. I couldn't even go in, it upset me so much."

"Has she ever done this before?"

"No, not her. Never."

"Perhaps she had a party?"

"Remember I told you we lost our sweet baby recently? We don't have anything to party about."

Yosef sighed. "My heart aches with yours about the baby. You must have been devastated…. Both of you."

"I was. We are still. It's torn our marriage apart."

"And you were headed home tonight, in great hope of beginning to rebuild."

"Yes, until I saw the booze bottles."

"You've been hurt before by someone's drinking?"

Now Kevin looked at Yosef, as if seeing him for the first time. Perhaps as if seeing himself for the first time. "My mother was an alcoholic. It devastated my Dad. She left. He raised me. No way am I letting myself in for that torture."

Their lemonades arrived but neither man drank.

Finally, Yosef turned on his swivel stool and faced Kevin. "Losing a child is a terribly painful experience, one neither parent can recover from without time and courage and love."

"I was her father. My job was to protect her." His throat rumbled as he tried to clear the constriction there. "I failed her."

"It sounds like your wife needs protecting now."

Kevin shook his head. "No offense, but women in this generation don't want protection. They take self-defense classes. Assertiveness training. Body building. They don't want or need rescuing by men nowadays."

"Maybe she doesn't need physical protection, but it sounds like her heart needs protecting while it heals, and I bet you are the one that can do that."

Kevin considered the idea but then said, "She threw me out."

"She invited you back. Where are the flowers and pizza?"

"I tossed them into the recycle bin with the bottles. Yosef, I can't deal with an alcoholic."

He didn't tell Yosef that upon seeing the bottles he had stalked back to his truck and grabbed the baseball bat he had bought as soon as he had heard his wife was pregnant, the one he'd given to his tiny baby Rosette when she was born. He had returned to the recycle crate and smashed every liquor bottle, swinging the bat like a sledgehammer until he shattered his anger along with the glass. He sat on the porch then and buried his face in his hands, allowing himself to finally cry for his lost little girl and the death of his dreams. He didn't tell Yosef any of this but suspected the man could see it in his face when he looked at him with those gentle brown eyes.

Yosef rested his hand on Kevin's shoulder. "Kevin, she isn't your mother, and you aren't a child anymore. She might need you to help her get back on track, and if that isn't enough, you can find her the help she needs. She's broken hearted. She needs you, and she's worth it."

Kevin inhaled deeply, nodded, and stood. "Thank you, Yosef. You're right. She is worth it. I'll go see her. I'm too drained tonight, but soon."

Kevin left, and moments later, Yosef paid and walked out of the diner. On the sidewalk, Miriam slid her arm into his. Yosef looked at her and grinned.

"You're a good man, Yosef," she said. "How was the desert?"

"Still beautiful in its own way. It made me nostalgic. I missed having you on my donkey."

Miriam nudged his shoulder with hers and chuckled. "I appreciate what you did in the desert, and here as well."

Yosef offered her the to-go cup he'd asked for and taken out with him. "You've got to try this. Ice in something called lemonade. What a gift!"

Jacquie had heard the commotion in her yard and peered out from behind the drapes. She watched in horror as her husband vented more anger than she'd ever seen in him, beating her empty alcohol bottles into oblivion. When he stopped, when he sat on the porch and wept, every fiber in her body said to go and comfort him. She didn't. His anger had immobilized her. She knew about his mother's alcoholism, though he hadn't talked much about her, and suddenly realized that her brief indulgence into drinking was the worst way she could have chosen to hurt him. She was too ashamed to go to him. Yet, something thawed inside her to finally see he, too, was struggling with his emotions. He had demonstrated, though in a shocking way, all the anger, bitterness, and fear that cohabited with her grief as well.

He stormed off in his truck before she could move.

Later, when she managed to pull herself together enough to sweep up the glass, she found the flowers and pizza.

She raised her eyes to the stars. "Please give us another chance to work this out," she prayed.

Night Shift

Miriam slipped into a darkened room in the nursing home. "Hello, Sandy, I'm Miriam. Would you like a visitor?"

"Why did you call me Sandy?" The voice of the middle-aged woman belied her years. She sounded ancient and weak. "I'm Didi."

"You go by Didi, and you have for many years, but your name is Sandy." Miriam held no judgment for the woman, simply compassion.

"How do you know?" Sandy sounded frightened. "Are you police? Are they still looking for me? I thought a hospital was a safe place to leave—"

"Be at peace, Sandy. More than 20 years have passed. Your Gloria is an adult now, with a delightful four-year-old daughter of her own. And an infant son. You have grandchildren."

A wounded-animal groan came from the woman. "I've missed so much."

"They are loved. Gloria is married to a good man."

"Does she know, Miriam? Does she know I had to leave her? I wasn't good for her." Quick gasps interspersed her words. "I couldn't take care of myself, ...let alone a child. Yes, I left her but... out of love. Hardest thing I've ever done. I still don't know... whether it was the right thing. I wanted her to be safe."

Sandy shook her head sadly. "I've ached for her... every day since then," she said. "Both of them."

"She doesn't know yet, Sandy, but I'll make sure she does before long."

"Tell them... I've always loved them," the woman said, before slipping into sleep, a temporary escape from a life filled with struggle, but which had been brightened by two soul-wrenching sacrifices.

CHAPTER 10

The next morning Gloria woke feeling troubled. She had dreamed of searching in vain for her mother. Perhaps visiting Daniel's parents had brought her own lack of family to the surface of her subconscious. Miriam had been in the dream, but Gloria couldn't quite remember more than that.

Her phone vibrated with a call, so Gloria eased out of the bed she stilled shared with Winnie and went into the living room. "Hello?"

"Mrs. Walters? This is Chaplain Murphy again. I have good news."

Gloria relaxed a bit. Early calls always threatened bad news, considering the line of work her husband was in, and a phone ringing always set her nerves on edge accordingly. She reminded herself he was safe and would soon arrive stateside, last she heard. "Good news about my husband?"

"Yes. The military hospital examined him. They will keep Captain Walters for a few days to begin some physical therapy, as one ankle was indeed broken and one badly sprained. But he should be home within a week."

"That's wonderful! Is he nearby? May I visit him?"

"I'm afraid they wouldn't say where he is, so I'd guess we will have to wait for him to come to you."

"Of course. I should have known better than to ask."

"I would have been surprised if you didn't. I would guess you can hardly wait to see for yourself that he is safe. I know you've had a rough time of it lately. Is there anything I can do for you in the meantime?"

"No, we are doing well enough, thank you. The other wives on base have been very kind."

"Please call me if you think of anything."

A week. Daniel would be home in a week. And though she'd never wish any harm to her husband, she couldn't help but be grateful that a broken ankle would keep him close to her for several more weeks, anyway.

She called Daniel's parents to share the news. They said they would come after he'd been home a couple of days so that the little family could have him to themselves for a bit. She appreciated their thoughtfulness and hoped again that Daniel would accept that she had welcomed them back into their lives. The more family the better, she felt. She had none for too many years of her life.

That thought reminded her of the dream and the mystery of her mother. She had exhausted every direction she had imagined in earlier years. Without knowing her mother's name or her own surname, without the police having been able to track her down all those years ago when her mother had abandoned her, she had nothing to go on.

The reporter came to mind and when 8:00 a.m. arrived, Gloria called Jacquie.

Her heart skipped a beat when Jacquie answered.

Gloria gave her the little news she knew, that her husband was at a military hospital and should be home in about a week. Jacquie thanked her and then asked, "Anything else?"

"Yes, actually. I wondered if you could help me with your research skills." Gloria quickly briefed Jacquie on her childhood. Having told the story to Henry made it easier to tell it again. "I just wondered if you had any ideas on how I could find her after all these years."

"Well, you're at a dead end without a name. Have you tried genetic testing? Even if your mother never had a test, you might match up with a relative who has, and they could have answers for you."

"Jacquie, that's a wonderful idea! I never thought of that."

"No guarantees, but lots of people are doing it now, so you never know."

Later that day on errands, Gloria found a kit for a DNA test at a pharmacy and within an hour had mailed it off. It would be hard to wait, both for Daniel and for results, but sunshine, blooming daffodils in the park, and hope lifted her spirits.

After talking to Gloria, Jacquie called Kevin's company office to learn where he would be working that day. All day at the newspaper desk she watched the clock and left a few minutes before Kevin would end his shift. When he came out of a half-finished house carrying his toolbox, she was waiting for him.

She watched his face when he noticed her, and it changed from smiling, to scowling, to impassive. He stopped a few feet from her and waited for her to speak.

"Hi, Kev," was all she could manage, though she'd rehearsed several different conversations.

He nodded.

"Can I take you to dinner?" She looked down at her feet, not wanting to see him reject her request. When he didn't answer, she met his eyes. "I'm sorry, Kevin. About throwing you out, about my drinking, about not being myself since..." She couldn't go on.

He set down the toolbox then and took her into his arms. "I'm sorry about the mess I made," he said into her hair. "I'm sorry about Rosette."

She cried, then, silently against his shoulder. "It wasn't your fault." She believed that now, and though the sadness didn't lift, perhaps a little of the anger diminished. "I watched you lose it with the bat last night, and somehow it made me feel a bit better. Like someone else could understand how close sadness and anger can be. I thought I was the only one, and that you were coping so well, and it made me angrier that you were coping when I wasn't."

He stepped back so they could look into each other's eyes. "Barely coping. I function okay at work, but I'm a mess when I'm not busy. I really need you. We need each other to get through this."

"So, dinner?" she asked again.

"Absolutely," he answered, and then kissed her tenderly.

Later, when they were back at home together, the two stood arm-in-arm looking into the nursery, both taking in the emptiness in the room as well as in their hearts. They needed time to heal, but perhaps they could do it together.

"We could try getting pregnant again," Kevin whispered, "but I can't handle it if you're drinking. You know my history with that, and I'm not willing to go through the chaos again.

"I don't want another baby," Jacquie answered as softly, "I want Rosette. I'm not ready to let go and move on, but I am ready to deal with my emotions without alcohol."

Kevin hugged her a little closer and nodded.

Night Shift

Miriam settled into a chair next to the bed of a 16-year-old boy. The hospital noises were subdued, for most patients were fast asleep at 2:00 a.m.

"Who's there?" the boy asked, his voice giving away his fear.

"Hi, Matthew. My name is Miriam. I'm a volunteer, and I work the night shift."

"Yeah, I figured it was night. The halls are quieter." He had relaxed a little.

"You're having trouble sleeping?"

"Yeah."

"Since the accident?"

"Yeah."

"Your uncle, Father Dave, tells me all about you. He says you've lost your sight. I'm very sorry. And yet you are being so brave."

"I guess." He turned toward her voice. "It's confusing, not being able to see whether it's day or night. I'm always awake. At least, it feels that way."

Miriam laid her hand on his. "And you're terribly bored when everyone else is asleep or busy?"

He sighed.

"Do you like dogs?"

"You mean, do I want a seeing eye dog?" His voice assured her he didn't.

"No, I just mean dogs in general. Do you like them?"

He nodded. "I miss my dog, Midnight."

"What kind is he?"

"Mostly Labrador, I think. Maybe something else in the mix."

"I have a friend with a black lab mix. He's a real character. In fact, one time," Miriam settled back in her chair and chuckled. "Well, let me start at the beginning. As a pup, he loved to steal socks and play with them. He'd growl and shake them, probably imagining they were great enemies. Then he'd toss them up in the air and pounce on them once they'd landed. Now my friend didn't appreciate finding her socks wadded up, soggy, and often quite holey, so she bought tennis balls for the dog and kept her socks hidden away.

"But the Lab wasn't disappointed, for now he had a prey that could roll and bounce. All the better, I'm sure he thought. And before long the dog had concocted all sorts of games with his tennis balls. One that my friend couldn't quite understand involved a laundry chute. You know what those are? Kind of a hole that lets you drop dirty clothes down to a laundry room below. Fascinating invention."

The boy nodded, and smiled, just a bit.

"The Lab started dropping the tennis ball down the laundry chute, watching it land, then tearing down the stairs to retrieve it!"

"My dog loves tennis balls, too!" Now the boy was grinning.

Miriam giggled. "But once on his way back up the stairs with it, the ball slipped out of his mouth, and of course, bounced all the way down. The dog's ears went up, and I think you could almost hear the gears in his head turning. For the rest of the day he would run up the stairs, drop the ball, nudge it if needed, and then chase it down the stairs."

The boy chuckled.

"But wait, that's not all!" Miriam said, laughing quietly, not wanting to wake anyone. "Yesterday I walked with my friend and her dog to the park. You aren't going to believe this, but it's true! When we got near the play structure, she let him off leash, and I figured she would toss him a ball, but no! As soon as the dog heard the leash unbuckle, ears flapping and tongue flopping, he sped towards the slide, ran up the steps as if he'd done this a thousand times and then hunkered down and slid down the slide!" Here she laughed so hard, still trying to be quiet, that she wrapped her arms around her sides to keep them from aching.

The boy too, couldn't keep his laughs in, whether from her story, or the sound of her trying to control her giggles.

When they had calmed, she explained, "My friend said it only took once watching his ball roll down the slide, and he was hooked. Now he doesn't even need the ball. He runs up the steps, glides down the slide without a moment's hesitation, and then does it all again as fast as he can. She doesn't dare take him off his leash if children are playing. She's afraid he'd bowl them over!"

The boy smiled broadly now, looking up at a ceiling he couldn't see, but clearly imagining the scene for himself. "I'll have to try that with my dog," he finally said.

Miriam chatted with him for another hour until he drifted off to sleep. As she left, she stopped at the nurses' station. "Hello, Meagan," she said to one, who didn't look surprised since she wore a nametag.

She did look very surprised a moment later, however, when Miriam said, "You know that little electronic piano keyboard that's in your car waiting to be donated? I bet Matthew, your patient in room 231 would love playing around with that. He could use the headphones so that he doesn't disturb anyone. It might help him be less bored. Oh, and thank you for the work you all do here with the children!"

Miriam walked toward the elevators, leaving one big-hearted nurse still at a loss for words.

CHAPTER 11

The next day Gloria's phone rang with a call from Daniel! He sounded a bit drugged, his speech slower than usual.

"Hi, Love, it's me."

"Daniel! It's wonderful to hear your voice. I was so very worried!"

"I'm okay. I'm just out of some surgery that they decided my ankle needed. Doc will be in to tell me how it went soon. How much do you know?"

"Chaplain Murphy called me first to say they had lost you, then found you, and then that you were at a hospital and would be home in about a week. He mentioned your ankles."

"One busted, one sprained, like I thought. I'll be good as new in a few weeks."

"How did it happen, or can you tell me?"

He went on to tell her about the plane going down, his long army crawl through the desert, though he didn't say which desert, and the man Yosef who saved his life.

The memory came to Gloria's mind of Miriam's prayer for Daniel's safety days ago, just before the soldiers knocked on her door.

Gloria squared her shoulders, ready to admit to Daniel that she had contacted his parents, but he interrupted her. "I have to go, honey. The surgeon just came in. I love you! I'll see you soon!" Then he had disconnected.

Ack! So many questions still unanswered. So much left unsaid. She sighed, setting the unknown aside, and turned to the very present needs of her children.

Ever since Miriam asked Henry to help anyone who asked, he had been trying to figure out how best to do that. She was right that assisting others brought meaning to his life, something he had missed since retiring and losing his wife. He so enjoyed Gloria's visits, and like he had told her, he considered working in a school to help children struggling with their reading or signing up to be a Big Brother. Yet, as much as Gloria's little ones entertained him, he wondered if volunteering with children would ease or exacerbate the grief of losing his only grandchild. Though he did have skills in helping people learn to read, maybe it should be adults he offered to assist.

He made a list of his skills and the activities he truly enjoyed. What had always brought him a sense of vibrance had been his work as an entrepreneur. Seeing a new project through to fruition invigorated him. Coordinating with others toward a common goal enriched everyone. He wished he could reexperience that sense of energy and revitalization. Was he too old, too burned out, to start anew?

"Mary, …Miriam," he prayed, "please ask your Son to bring me a project that will serve others and lighten this heavy heart."

Night Shift

Bone weary, a woman not yet 38 rocked a screaming infant in an effort to calm the little one. The woman felt no calm herself, for in her heart there was only room for grief and anger. Her 17-year-old daughter had died in the effort of bearing this child, and the baby now suffered the agony of drug withdrawal. The woman wanted to scream along with this tiny new grandson. She felt too young to be a grandmother. Too old to raise her daughter's child. She didn't know how much longer she could sit here in the hospital nursery and rock a baby who writhed and arched his back and seemed to fight her embrace.

A woman approached her, holding out her arms. "May I?" she asked.

The young grandmother relinquished the child with a mixture of relief and guilt. The woman, dressed in simple clothes, swayed side to side and hummed to the child.

"He hasn't quieted since he was born," the grandmother said.

"There's a recliner in the corner." The volunteer gestured toward it with her head. "You rest, and I'll cuddle him a while. You've been through enough and deserve a little sleep."

The grandmother nodded, and though the baby didn't calm, she felt herself loosen her tight hold on her anger. She sank into the recliner and into a moment of gratitude that broke through the grief. As she closed her eyes, she envisioned the nursery volunteer silhouetted against a star-lit sky, rocking her grandson in one arm as she hummed a gentle tune. The grandmother opened her eyes and was still in the hospital nursery across from the gentle woman, who indeed was rocking her crying grandson in one arm. She closed her eyes again and was back in the night scene, but this time the woman's other arm felt like a gentle support around her back. They swayed together as they watched the sky. Northern lights played across the horizon, the same northern lights she had seen at one of the happiest moments of her childhood. The lights' undulation became one with the rocking of the baby and the swaying of the two women. Her spirit rose with the aurora waves and she experienced a sense of gratitude and joy beyond any she'd ever known. She relaxed into the feeling, knowing there was a God, knowing that He loved her beyond measure and had an unfathomable but beautiful plan.

The new grandmother awoke several hours later. Miriam was still near her in the nursery gently rocking her grandson, who now slept peacefully. She hadn't noticed before how much he looked like her daughter had when she was born. The woman's heart softened with love and a tender protectiveness. The loss was still there and with it a deep sadness, but love had begun to contain her pain.

After settling the baby in his grandmother's outstretched arms, Miriam returned to watch the dancing northern night sky. Though it was dark there and had been for months now, if people were near, they could have made out the figure of a woman in a long parka, her head thrown back in delight as she watched the sky. As it was, only caribou witnessed her sit on a snow drift and begin to rock, as if in a fine upholstered chair. A backdrop of dancing light that reached from the horizon to heaven itself silhouetted the woman. Greens, yellows, and an occasional shimmer of red formed pulsing streams that brightened and dimmed, shrank and grew, undulated and paused above her. Beauty, goodness, and faith were one within her. She raised her arms and swayed, for the movement in the sky demanded participation. The aurora was one of Miriam's favorite experiences of earth's nature. How good God was to create such a delight for the senses.

Her lap now supported a sphere, much like it had before her Child was born. She wrapped her arms around it in a gentle embrace and rocked all of the earth, all of humanity, as she comforted each person's pain, shared their joy, and echoed their prayers of gratitude. If the caribou had watched and dared to blink, they would have missed the moment when she had gone. Yet many of her children would feel she was still with them, still embracing them, attentive to each of their stories.

CHAPTER 12

Five more days passed as Gloria tried to stay busy to make the time go faster until Daniel returned. With her in-laws deciding not to come until their son was home, she had moved back to her own bed, realizing it wouldn't be good for Winnie to get used to not sleeping alone. She hoped the smoky smell of the beds had dissipated, though possibly she was simply becoming accustomed to it.

When the insurance check arrived, she deposited it and drove immediately to buy new mattresses for her children. She was grateful for the furniture that came with the apartment, even though the sofa and chair showed wear and the kitchen table wobbled. She counted it as a blessing that she didn't need to immediately replace all the furniture ruined by glass shards. She would wait to buy a new mattress for their double bed until Daniel was home and could help her choose a firmness he liked. Or maybe its acrid smokiness would be completely gone by then.

The same five days passed for Jacquie as she tried to resume the comfort level she and Kevin used to share. Their conversations weren't as strained as they had been, and he still hadn't pressed her to make love, though she treasured the consolation of having him in her bed again. There seemed to be an unspoken agreement between them that she would initiate when she was ready.

If ever.

At least, she hoped they both mutually understood.

Jacquie continued to search for the Miriams. She felt fairly confident that she had hit on the answer to her confusion. The Miriams were all members of some group that helped people in any way they could, but the name Miriam gave them anonymity. It didn't quite explain the various descriptions of the Explosion Miriam who had accompanied Gloria to the clinic, but perhaps that was simply a result of how busy nurses can be. If that weren't the answer, she'd have to accept her father's claim that Miriam was the Grocery Mary from his childhood, whom he thought was the Virgin Mary, which was impossible to believe.

She spent her free hours interviewing the people who had responded to her request in the paper to tell her stories of Miriams who had helped them. So far, she'd talked to a teen who claimed Miriam helped her deliver her baby under a stoop, a nun who believed she was given a new ministry with help from a Miriam, a blind teen who said a Miriam visited him in the middle of the night in the hospital. One Lieutenant Meyers said a woman named Miriam had called her office to tell them about an army wife who needed resettling onto the base. Before that call the lieutenant had been feeling discouraged about her work and had wondered how it served her country. Bringing the wife, her children, and the few possessions they could salvage to a new home made her proud to be doing her part. Jacquie assumed that the Miriam who called the army base was probably Explosion Miriam calling about her friend Gloria.

Then there were the countless stories of people who said a woman had helped them, though she hadn't told them her name. She wanted to ignore those accounts, for there was no evidence that the helpers were also calling themselves Miriam, yet the stories grabbed her imagination. A man whose father had died, met by a consoling woman on a mountain trail in the dark. An old priest comforted by an elderly female stranger in a moment of great sadness. A grandmother who said a woman not only held her screaming new grandson all night after he was born addicted, but somehow brought a sense of peace and acceptance to the grandma. An elderly man who had died smiling after telling his daughter that Mother Mary came. "Miriam is a form of the name Mary," the daughter had insisted when Jacquie interviewed her.

In the end, she wrote a lengthy article about the many appearances of helpful Miriams and her conclusion that they were all loosely related by some agreement to call themselves Miriam while helping others, in order to maintain anonymity. She dubbed the group the Myriad Miriams.

After five days of phone silence, Daniel finally called and told Gloria what time he would arrive at the airport. She, Winnie, and Peter all dressed as if for Easter and were waiting for him at Security when an airport employee wheeled him through to them. Winnie flew onto his lap, which made Daniel grin, and Gloria's heart sing.

He looked a bit gaunt and still sunburned from his time in the desert.

"Welcome home," she said when Winnie had settled down. She kissed him on the lips and then thanked the attendant with a tip. "I'll take it from here," she said to the man, and then to Daniel, "Do you have any gear to get at baggage claim?"

"Not a thing," her husband answered. "The only things that made it back were what I was wearing. Be thankful the hospital washed them for me, or you wouldn't be smiling to see me right now. You'd be standing ten feet back."

"Lost a little sweat in the desert?"

"More than a little."

"I guess we're meeting you with considerably less in the way of belongings than when you left, too. Half a house less."

"As long as you three are here, that's all that matters."

"Ditto," she said, and gave him another kiss before she started to push him toward the parking garage.

In a way, though, she did have more than when he left. She had a bigger family. She had parents-in-law and she didn't know how Daniel would feel about that. He had asked her to wait. Well, they could talk about that when they got home, while kids were napping, she figured.

No sooner had she decided to wait than Winnie piped up. "Daddy!" said the four-year-old, "I have a new Grandma and Grandpa!"

Gloria stopped pushing the wheelchair. She should have realized Winnie would want to share what was new in her life.

Daniel turned to look back at Gloria. "Oh?" His eyebrows lifted.

Gloria started to push the chair again. "I started to tell you about that right when you had to get off the phone in the hospital."

Winnie wasn't to be stopped. "Their names are Grandma Margo and Grandpa Pete. You should meet them, they're really nice."

Gloria sighed. "Winnie, sweetie, Daddy knows them. They're his parents, remember?"

"Oh yeah. Aren't they nice, Daddy? And there's Mr. Martin. He's really nice, too, and he lets me play at his house while he and Mama give each other lessons."

"Sounds like I've missed quite a bit in the days I've been gone."

Gloria heard the question behind the strain in her husband's voice.

"Mr. Martin is an elderly friend of Miriam's," she explained to Daniel. "He's helping me with my reading, and I'm teaching him to cook. He's a recent widower."

Gloria was relieved to arrive at the car. She could explain so many things later. They'd have time to talk, weeks of it, and she said a quick prayer of gratitude for all the time ahead that they might not have had. After stowing his army-issued wheelchair in the back of the minivan, she went around to the driver's side of the car and felt a bit of relief that her husband had gotten in on the passenger side. The results of the explosion only showed from her side and were rather frightening, she realized. Another thing to explain. The car shop had replaced broken windows but hadn't scheduled the body work yet. Errands like that would be easier now, with Daniel home to help.

She decided to drive him past their old house on the way to the base. Might as well start at the beginning.

Daniel gave a low whistle as they parked in front of what remained of their house.

The home across the street from theirs had been leveled and removed, but the blackened remains of foundation and cellar looked like an ominous, gaping entrance to hell. A jolt ran up his back, and he realized how easily he could have lost his whole family. Their own house had construction fencing around it to keep the curious out. He could see why. Very little remained to support the upper floor. He, and anyone who passed by, could see into their kitchen, half bath, and living room—the whole main floor, actually. The upstairs still held some semblance of privacy, and his mind wandered to how it had been before. Two little bedrooms that had been their own safe harbors from the world.

Gloria pointed to the upstairs window and described again how Miriam had climbed to help her and Winnie down.

"Where was Peter?" Daniel asked, his voice a bit trembly.

She told him about buckling him into the car, then running back into the house to take Winnie to the bathroom, and how she had insisted on using the upstairs bathroom. Daniel shot a sincere thank-you prayer heavenward.

"I've seen houses like this before," he said. "In other countries. War torn countries. The remains after bombing."

Relieved he hadn't berated her for leaving their son alone in the car, she knew she had admonished herself countless times already.

"Some people thought it was a bomb at first," she answered.

"I can see why," was all he said. But he reached his hand across the seat of the car and held onto hers. "I almost lost you."

"We almost lost you, too." Her voice cracked and she cleared her throat. He knew she wanting to appear strong. She was like that, always trying to be a brave military spouse. But this, this was more than any wife should have had to bear alone.

"Mama," a voice from the backseat ventured. "I don't want to see the house anymore. It's scary now. Daddy, will you fix it for us?"

"I will, sweetheart. Or I'll get us a new one."

"The soldiers and Mama did that," Winnie answered.

"Your mama did an amazing job of keeping you safe," Daniel said, and squeezed Gloria's hand again. "I'm proud of you all."

Daniel struggled with guilt for not being home during the rest of the drive to the base and their apartment. When Gloria told him about Lieutenant Meyers arriving at the scene ready to move the little family into a new home, he made a mental note to thank her. He was especially grateful to hear their new apartment was on the ground floor. Getting out of the wheelchair and into the car had been a challenge, but up a flight of steps would have been beyond them both.

The guard at the gate saluted when they stopped and said, "Welcome back, Captain Walters. Good to see you, sir."

He waved them through, and Gloria said to Daniel, "I feel a new sense of safety living on base where others are nearby to protect and help me. Thank God, my husband is home now, too."

He wanted to be her help and protection, but how could he like this? Daniel stuffed down his embarrassment as his wife pushed him in his wheelchair into their apartment. He carried Peter on his lap, and Winnie ran ahead to point to each room and give him the tour.

"I smell the smoke," he said, as soon as he was in.

"I'm sorry. I've replaced the kids' mattresses, but I think ours will have to go, too. I waited so we could choose it together."

"I didn't mean to sound critical. It's simply hitting me all that you've been through."

"When you were missing, it put all that in perspective. We lost things. That's nothing compared to if we had lost you."

Yes, they only lost things, but they nearly lost their lives. How would he have gone on without his family?

He had nothing to unpack or put away, so they settled at the kitchen table and Gloria made macaroni and cheese for the kids. She had bought two small steaks to celebrate Daniel coming home, and he told her they were the best he'd ever eaten. The desert goat's milk and the bland hospital meals had left him ready for red meat.

Winnie's chatter filled any awkward silence at the table, and after her third mention of Miriam, he interrupted.

"Gloria," he said before Winnie could start another story, "did Miriam ever mention someone named Yosef?"

"Not that I remember."

He told her then about Yosef, his rescuer, the goat's milk, and the long ride in the dark. He talked about the donkey ears that stayed down as long as they were in danger. He described the tender kindness of the man who had seemed to know right where he was, though the desert was unlit even by moonlight before he found him.

"He said Miriam sent him to me."

"My Miriam, do you think?"

"I wondered that, too, for a second, but how could that be?"

How could a nomad in some desert be married to a woman in the States? And how would she have known where Daniel was? He never even told Gloria where he was deployed. It must simply be a common name, Miriam. Yet, how could any Miriam know where he was in the dark in the desert?

Jacquie couldn't believe the response she had been receiving from her recent article about what she called the Myriad Miriams. Though no one claimed to be part of a group of women who spread acts of kindness under the alias of Miriam, countless women seemed ready to start groups like the one she thought already existed. They loved the name Myriad Miriams and each day she heard from women whose friends or coworkers were ready to reach out to the needy anonymously. After the printing of her article, each day brought more reports to her email of secret deeds completed with the sole purpose of helping people. Some called them works of mercy, others, acts of charity. It wasn't what Jacquie had intended. Now she'd likely never know if the original Miriams were actually a group of different women or not. Still, she couldn't help but feel good about what she had accidentally begun.

Daniel had trouble sleeping that night. He kept waking from terrible dreams brought on, he knew, by the sight of his own house wrecked by an explosion. He'd seen dozens of such explosions. Each time was a traumatic climax of tense situations, but the owners usually no longer occupied their homes. In this one, however, it wasn't possible to emotionally detach himself from the loss that a family suffers when their house is destroyed.

Those nightmares seemed interspersed with dreams of crawling through an endless desert. These, too, were all too real. He had forgotten to tell Gloria to leave the wheelchair at his bedside in case he needed to get up during the night. It was across the room, out of reach, making him feel all the more trapped, without an escape.

They had talked late into the night, each sharing the challenges they'd faced. He had kept one challenge back, however. In the hospital, when he'd cut off the call with Gloria, the surgeon had come to tell him that his fall had shattered his ankle. He'd be able to walk again, thanks to the surgery and with physical therapy, but never without a limp. He would probably have to serve his country from behind a desk, if his military career could continue at all.

That was why he hadn't called Gloria during the remaining days in the hospital. He didn't know what their future would hold. What kind of work would he do if he left the army? He'd already put in ten years, but that wasn't enough for an early retirement.

Yet another thought kept him awake. His parents. Gloria had visited them, and it sounded like they'd warmed to her once they met the grandchildren. But could he forgive them for not welcoming her into the family earlier? For not coming to their wedding? For not being there when his children were born?

They could have helped Gloria when the house collapsed. They could have comforted her when she heard he was missing. Instead they had distanced themselves when he told them he had fallen in love, and they wouldn't even meet her once they learned she had no family, education, or upbringing.

Did he still even love them?

But he remembered Yosef's strange, unsettling words to him, "You need to get back to your wife and two little ones." He had looked pointedly at Daniel. "And reconcile with your parents." Had he been delirious and mentioned his children earlier? Or was he delirious when he heard Yosef's advice? He hadn't thought so. And he really doubted he'd have mentioned his estrangement from his parents. Daniel also pondered Yosef's parting instructions as he was carried to the helicopter, "Go love your family, carrying peace in your heart. Go with God."

How could he carry peace in his heart, if he couldn't forgive?

Night Shift

In the still, dark hours of early morning, Miriam settled onto the front porch step of a group home for children who awaited adoption. Many of the residents were teens who had given up on a forever family to love them. Now they simply put in the days until they would age out and be responsible for themselves. Normally a naturally joyful person, tonight Miriam felt deep sorrow because she knew inside the house two different girls silently had cried themselves to sleep. She also ached as she sensed resentment grow in a young man who had hardened his heart and learned not to cry. She wept the tears he would not, for him and for every child who felt unwelcome. If only they could know how much their Heavenly Father treasured each of them personally.

Her thoughts turned to other unwanted, unloved children, tiny bodies yet unborn. She ached for those who would fall to abortion and wept even more for their families. Other unborn treasures had families who desperately wanted them, but would die and be miscarried, piercing the hearts of parents who yearned to hold the little ones in their arms. Tears filled her eyes, spilled over, and rolled down Miriam's cheeks. She inhaled a shaky breath and then began to sob. Her head bowed; her shoulders shook. She rocked with her grief, as women rock in prayer at the Wailing Wall.

Both types of babies would join the angels and know true happiness in heaven, but the families would have missed out on the love they would have experienced from and for each little soul. It was heartbreaking to her that any child would not know the joy of a mother's warm embrace and the pride of a father's gaze.

She had loved her own Son so very much. When He was dying and transferred her care to John, He also gave her to the world. From that moment, she held immeasurable love for each of the Father's children and treasured them truly as her own.

This night, like the day when her Son died, the Father comforted her by bestowing on her the gift of Motherhood to every person. She prized each child who lived in this group home as if that child were her only child. She would request graces for them so that tomorrow each would awaken with renewed hope and a sense of worth. And for the unborn, Miriam stepped out of time and space. She spiritually cuddled and rocked each infant on its journey from this world. She carried each tiny person, one by one, directly into the lovingly awaiting arms of the Father of All. She couldn't remain sad, having witnessed the way He cherished each of His own. With a deep inhale and exhale, she let the sorrow go, and He renewed her joy.

CHAPTER 13

Jacquie kissed Kevin goodbye and hurried to her car. She felt a glimmer of the enjoyment her job brought her on days like today, and the distraction felt like a gift. Gloria had called and offered to have Jacquie come meet her husband and interview him for her newspaper.

It was midmorning by the time Jacquie made it through Portland rush hour traffic and arrived at the little apartment at the army base. Gloria, with Winnie helping hold the door, welcomed her inside. She immediately noticed a lightness to Gloria that hadn't been there before. Probably not since her house trouble. Maybe not since her husband went on his assignment. Gloria had forewarned her that he couldn't talk about his mission, but there was plenty of story available, she was sure.

"Jacquie Perdue, this is my husband, Daniel," Gloria had said.

Jacquie had scanned the visible rooms, relieved not to see Gloria's baby. He was too close to the age her Rosette would have been, and she knew her emotions might get the best of her if he were in sight. He must be napping. She pulled her attention back to Gloria's last words and turned to meet Gloria's Daniel. She hadn't been prepared to see him in a wheelchair but recovered quickly. "Nice to meet you, uh, Captain Walters."

"Daniel is just fine, *Mrs.* Perdue," he emphasized her formal title with humor in his voice, and she immediately liked him.

"Jacquie is just fine for me, too. I hear you've been through the wringer, so to speak."

He nodded and told her what story that he could, beginning with his airplane losing control and his men parachuting.

"I know I can't ask where and why, but did the other men get home safely?"

"All who parachuted off the plane before me were recovered safely. I jumped after my men." He answered with a tone that she understood to mean not to ask the obvious next questions. Was someone on the plane who couldn't jump off? Had a member of their group died?

"Tell me about your rescue," she continued, hoping that was safe enough.

As he told her about Yosef, her head began to spin a little, and she was glad that there was no alcohol to blame. Yosef. Her own husband had told her about meeting a Yosef at the diner. First Miriams were coming out of the woodwork. Would Yosefs, too? Such an unusual name. Could this all be a hoax?

When Daniel said, "He told me Miriam sent him," she stood up suddenly. This was too much. She looked to Gloria who shrugged.

"We don't understand it either," she said.

Forgetting all professionalism, Jacquie plopped down in the chair again. "My husband has just told me about meeting a man named Yosef in our local diner." She could hear the incredulity in her voice, but she continued. "A man in his 50s maybe, with loose fitting hippy kind of clothes, dark brown trim beard shot with grey, Jewish appearance and accent?"

"My Yosef wore a loose robe like a nomad, otherwise, similar description."

"When did you last see him?"

"I left him and his donkey near a desert cave seven days ago."

"And I can assume it wasn't a desert in the U.S.?"

Daniel didn't answer, but Jacquie knew he had been airlifted to a military hospital that wasn't near enough for Gloria to visit, so no, probably not this country.

"My husband spoke with his Yosef seven nights ago in person at the diner near our home."

"So, it couldn't be the same man," Daniel concluded.

"Right, of course," Jacquie agreed, but something told her it wasn't that simple.

While trying to understand Daniel's story, Jacquie heard the baby cry and her excruciating yearning for Rosette replaced every thought.

106

"Oops, nap time is over, I guess," Gloria said as she rose and started toward the hallway.

Jacquie panicked. She didn't want to see the baby who was too much a reminder of her own loss. She stood quickly, saying, "That's my cue to leave you to your family, Daniel. Congratulations on your safe return." With that she fled out the door before either Gloria or Daniel could invite her to stay longer.

She pushed her yearning for Rosette out of her mind on the ride back to her condo, and instead mulled over Daniel's story. She stayed focused on that once home and immediately wrote and submitted her article. It was a good story even without the Yosef question included or resolved. Sarge would be pleased with it.

With her article sent off, Jacquie had no more defenses to distract her from the way she had reacted to Peter's cry at Gloria and Daniel's house. What must they think of her, the way she practically flew out of their house? She owed them an explanation.

Still sitting at her computer, she composed a note to Gloria:

Dear Gloria and Daniel,
   Forgive the way I left your home so suddenly. We recently lost a baby who would have been about Peter's age...

Suddenly she couldn't see the screen anymore through the tears that rose in her eyes and then spilled out to trail down her cheeks. How long, Lord? How long will it hurt this much? When will I be normal again?

She slammed the laptop closed, stood up, and busied herself with making a special dinner for Kevin. That night she didn't share her grief, but instead she told Kevin all about Daniel's story and the uneasy feeling she had about the multiple Miriams and the two Yosefs.

Kevin looked at her, and the way he lowered his voice gave her goosebumps. "My Yosef mentioned having been in the desert, saying that was why he ordered lemonade."

Night Shift

A woman named Esther sat alone in her room, her first evening in the new "senior living home" her children had chosen for her. She didn't want to be here. She wanted her own house, her own bed, her own walls that contained 50 years of memories. Realizing she was courting resentment and determined to stay positive, she decided to walk and explore some of the common areas in order to distract herself.

A Catholic organization ran the home. She and all her family were Jewish. She knew they'd chosen this home because it was equidistant to their three homes, but Catholic? How would she ever fit in?

She came to the little in-house theater and quite a few residents were entering. "What's playing?" she asked.

"The Cardinal," answered one lady who wore a large crucifix around her neck. "It's old but a classic."

And Catholic, Esther thought. Like everything else here but me.

She walked toward a quiet humming she heard and found a woman alone, rocking in a small room with two or three tables and several easy chairs. The woman seemed young for the home, but one never knew what type of illness might require assisted living. She wore a long skirt and a modest veil around her head. It reminded Esther of the head coverings that some of her more conservative friends wore. The woman saw her and stopped humming. She smiled at Esther and motioned her into the room.

Esther liked something about her smile and joined her. "I heard you humming. It sounded like a song from…" She was going to say synagogue but didn't know if she wanted to identify herself as an outsider just yet.

The woman grinned. "Sing with me! If there are any like us, they'll come. And if they don't know the songs, they'll come for the food!"

The woman gestured toward one of the tables, and Esther couldn't believe her eyes. Four different desserts filled the table, and not just any desserts, but pastries that looked identical to what her mother used to make for Passover or Hanukah years ago. There were crescent-shaped *rugelach*, cinnamon braided *babka* breads, triangular *hamantaschen* cookies, and *sufganiyot*, Esther's favorite little strawberry filled donuts.

"I'm Miriam," the younger woman said. "I'm a visitor, but I think we will find there are residents who will enjoy our treats." She began to sing then, and Esther was amazed. She sang with the same accent her mother never had lost, even though she had emigrated as a teenager and spent almost 70 years in America.

Esther sang along, quietly first but then, encouraged by the joy and strength of Miriam's voice, she sang Hava Nagila with gusto. Next Miriam began Dayeinu, one of Esther's favorite songs from Seder celebrations.

Two women peeked into the room and then, after their eyes widened at the sight of the treat table, entered and joined in the song. They were quite a choir now, and someone in the theater across the hall closed the door to keep out their noise. Laughing, they kept singing as first one, then two more men shyly entered and joined their voices to the group. They sang songs of faith and family and difficult times. They connected through their sung history, their eyes saying, "You, too? I didn't know."

Miriam changed to a soft, reverent *Shema Yisrael* and her little choir responded with tears in their eyes and emotion in their voices. When the song ended, the little group began to introduce themselves or tell their stories. They were still visiting when the movie across the hall finished, and they invited other friends to come enjoy some delicious treats with them.

What had been quiet, unshared backgrounds now emerged as points of pride and opened the way for telling treasured stories. The Jewish elderly became a small community, welcomed within a larger community. The residents raved about the evening so much that the chef promised to try the recipes found under each serving tray. Soon cultural singalongs and desserts became a regular event.

Esther made many new friends that night, but somehow Miriam had slipped away before she was able to thank her. No one else seemed to have seen her or knew which resident she might have been visiting.

CHAPTER 14

Gloria and Daniel sat in their little living room, both deep in thought. Winnie was on the rug entertaining her little brother with her dolls. Daniel hadn't said more about Gloria having gone to visit his parents, but she knew her time was running out.

"I thought your parents should know you were missing," she said, sounding apologetic even to herself.

"I understand," he said but didn't add more.

She took a deep breath. "They are coming to visit. Today. I received a text about an hour ago."

His answering scowl was not the face she had hoped to see. But then he relaxed. "That's okay. I don't want to leave our relationship like this. If I had died over there, we wouldn't have had a chance to fix things."

"They were good to me and the kids, even though we showed up unannounced. I think Winnie and Peter melted their hearts."

She checked Peter's diaper, and Daniel reached for her to hand him his son. "I can definitely understand this guy melting hearts." Then he blew a raspberry into Peter's tummy and received the smiles the maneuver always brought. Winnie ran over to join the fun and he tickled her until she jumped back out of reach.

"How long will you need the wheelchair?" Gloria asked, since they were already broaching difficult subjects. He hadn't let her help him much the last two mornings, insisting on dressing himself. She didn't know how he managed in the bathroom, but she knew he was determined to do as much as he could.

"Possibly six weeks. By then both ankles should be healing." He looked away from Gloria, and she realized there was more.

"Daniel?"

He met her gaze. "The sprain is serious and still won't take my weight. The break is bad. Even with the surgery and cast, I'm not likely to walk without a limp."

She saw the disappointment in his eyes and went to him. Lifting their son, she settled Peter back on his blanket on the floor and returned to Daniel. She knelt in front of him and held both his hands. "And?"

"No more Special Forces for me." His voice broke, just a little, on the last word, and he cleared his throat. "I'll meet with my superiors tomorrow and know more about my future after that. Possibly they'll offer me a training or desk job to fill out the months left on my tour of duty."

She could tell from the way he said it that he hated the idea. He really loved his missions and the comradery of his soldiers.

"They might suggest a medical discharge." He hung his head as if it were something to be ashamed of.

He leaned forward and kissed her. "I'm sorry I didn't call you from the hospital once I knew. I guess I needed a little time before I could talk about it."

He'd been in Special Forces even when she met him five years ago. She had no idea what other work he might be able to do. It seemed like one disaster after another was pummeling their family, from losing their home to possibly losing their income. Yet, her heart brimmed with gratitude to still have him and her children. Together, they'd make it.

A knock broke their silence.

Gloria jumped up to answer the door and welcomed her newfound in-laws. She embraced each of them in turn, and Winnie squealed, "Grandma Margo! Grandpa Pete!" and ran to them for her own hugs.

An awkward silence fell as the small group separated and they all looked at Daniel.

His father spoke first, "I'm mighty glad to see you, son." He walked to the wheelchair and extended his hand.

After a split-second hesitation that worried Gloria, Daniel reached for his father's hand and pulled him into a hug. His mother quickly followed suit, bending to hold her son in a long squeeze.

"I'm sorry," the three said in unison.

"We were wrong," Pete said. "Nothing should ever separate a family the way we let it." He gestured for Gloria to come to him, and he placed his arm around her shoulders. "We should have trusted you would choose a wonderful girl. And you have."

Gloria felt a warmth spread from her heart to her cheeks. Margo released her son's hand and turned to Gloria. With arms wide and mascara smeared, she hugged Gloria for as long as she'd hugged Daniel.

Finally, Gloria had parents. She felt like she might be literally glowing, the joy was so strong.

"To think of all we missed out on," Margo said, shaking her head. "Your wedding, your children's births." She pulled a tissue out of her pocket and wiped below her eyes. "We hope you'll let us make up for lost time. I don't want to ever miss a milestone again!"

Gloria looked to her husband and could see by the tightness of his jaw that he still had some way to go before he could forgive all, but they had taken the first difficult steps. She only wished her own family could have a chance like this, that she could find her mother and understand what had happened. How could a mom abandon a child? She looked from Peter as he worked to sit up on his blanket, to Winnie, pulling her grandfather over to read her one of the books Henry Martin had loaned them. She couldn't imagine leaving either of her children behind for any reason.

If she did find her mother, might that woman play on the floor with Peter, the way Grandma Margo now did, or read to Winnie with the same tenderness as Grandpa Pete?

A chilling thought suddenly occurred to her. Might Gloria wish instead that she had never introduced her children to the other grandma? The one who didn't care enough to enter the hospital with her burned four-year-old.

Later, when her in-laws had left, she talked about her hopes and fears for her family with Daniel. To her relief, he hadn't accused her of ambushing him with his parents' visit, and actually seemed appreciative. The hard feelings between him and his parents were behind them now and they could go forward without that mixed sense of self-righteousness and guilt that defined the family break.

"I wish…" She paused, not knowing quite what she wanted. "I wish

I could reconcile with my mother, too."

Daniel had stopped what he was doing and gave her his full attention. "I forget how hard your childhood was. You're such a great mom that it doesn't seem possible you didn't have a role model. I'm behind you in whatever you want to do. Every day that I spend with you and the kids now reinforces how important family is."

She told him about taking the DNA test that Jacquie had suggested. Maybe once she had results, she would know what the next step would be. Until then, she'd be grateful for her husband, her little ones, and now for Pete and Margo.

Later that night Gloria checked her email as she had been checking each night since she mailed in her test, waiting for her genetic results, though she had read it could take up to six weeks before contact. It wasn't so much that she wanted to know what percent of her heredity came from what country. She wanted to know why a common kitchen accident was enough to make her mother decide to abandon her.

She shook her head. How could a lab test give her those kinds of answers?

That same night, while Kevin and Jacquie watched television together on the couch, Kevin put his arm around her back and began to rub her upper arm gently. Jacquie could feel herself tense. She had enjoyed this touch many times before and knew where he intended it to lead. Tonight, she didn't want to enjoy it. She shifted slightly away from him and he stopped. Then, only a few minutes later, he moved his leg so that it was touching her from hip to ankle. So much for what she thought was a mutually agreed break from making love. She turned and looked at him.

"What?" he asked, his face all innocent.

She cocked her head and he sobered.

"I'd like to hold you. I'd like to make love again," he whispered.

She inhaled sharply, and realized at least partly she wanted him, too. But she really, really didn't want to be pregnant again yet, if ever. She couldn't bear experiencing this pain and loss again. She didn't really know where she was in her cycle. It was still too soon after the birth and nursing to judge.

Kevin shifted and kissed her in a way that made her toes curl.

Perhaps she could give in to the physical warmth that was spreading through her body. Maybe love making could, at least for a while, distract her from her pain. She returned his kiss and raised the ante.

He turned off the television and led her upstairs.

Night Shift

While it was still dark, before anyone unlocked the doors of a test lab and the early shift began, a slight woman with a blue veil selected one of the many DNA samples that had arrived the day before in the mail. Normally it would have waited its turn, and results would not be available for a good six weeks. But this sample found its way to the top of the pile, so the tests would be run on it today. The woman smiled, then was gone before anyone clocked in.

CHAPTER 15

Daniel woke early, needing more time now to get ready for duty. He was officially on medical leave, but his commanding officer had asked him to report to talk about his future. He turned his head to look at the wheelchair that now waited next to his bed. He hated it! He wanted to send it flying across the room, but he thought better of that. Where would he be without it? He despised what had happened to him, and though he knew he should be grateful to be alive—not all his men from that assignment had survived, he reminded himself—he would have given almost anything to be able to continue with the work he loved.

His colonel would already have the report from the surgeon and know that his Special Forces days were over. And what could be next? A desk job? His ankle was permanently damaged, but his energy and passion were still all-systems-go. He'd hate to sit daily behind a wooden barrier between him and people. He wanted to make a difference, bring a little more peace to the world from behind the scenes. It wasn't about glory. His assignments were always top secret and would remain uncelebrated, unknown to all but a very few, which was fine with him. He didn't need adulation. He needed meaning, to know that what he did made a difference. Was that all in his past now? He sighed and struggled out of bed and into his chair, then rolled himself to the bathroom.

He hoisted his body onto a shower chair, the kind used in nursing homes, feeling quite sorry for himself. It was not a familiar or welcome feeling. "Snap out of it," he said aloud. "Buck up!"

Gloria opened the bathroom door. "You okay?" She yawned, and his mood lifted. Just seeing her, though still half asleep and with her dark hair going every which way, he knew he was one lucky man. Not only was she beautiful, she was incredibly sweet and dedicated totally to him and the kids. He'd won the jackpot the day he walked into her diner.

He smiled back at her, his chest suddenly all warm and tight. "I'm fine. Great, actually."

She nodded and returned sleepily to her bed. Their bed. Hadn't she shown him how very whole and capable and lovable she thought he was, the first night he was back? And twice more since then. He grinned, in spite of himself, and began to count his blessings.

His disposition had improved greatly by the time he'd refreshed himself with a shower and dressed in his uniform. No sooner had he finished a breakfast spent laughing at the antics of his children than an aide knocked on their door, ready to drive him to see the colonel.

Within a few minutes, Daniel rolled into the office and straightened in his wheelchair as he saluted his commander, Colonel Small. Though the colonel's surname was unfortunate, for he stood barely 5'4", the man himself commanded respect both by his bearing and by his dedication to his troops. Daniel realized he looked up to the commander for more reasons than his confinement to a sitting position.

Colonel Small returned the salute, nodded, and said, "At ease, Captain Walters." He stood to shake Daniel's hand and then returned to his seat across the desk. "I can't tell you how relieved I am to have you back safely. I've read your debriefing. Sounds like both the mission and your rescue were harrowing."

"I'm grateful to be back, sir. Grateful to quite a few people, actually."

"Yes, I read about your experience with the nomad Yosef. We've searched for him to recognize him for the service he did for us, but he seems to have disappeared. No one knows who he is or where he lives."

"He didn't seem like the type who would want to be recognized. Just a simple man of faith who felt led to help me."

The colonel studied his desk for a few moments, then took a deep breath. Daniel wondered if the officer postponed performing a duty he didn't want to do. Was Daniel's career over? He waited.

"The surgeon's report is disappointing, Captain Walters."

Here it comes, Daniel thought and braced himself.

The colonel's face relaxed. "Daniel, you've served your country well for the last ten years. I thank you personally for all you've done. I know you aren't the kind of man who would welcome desk duty, so I'm going to give you a choice."

Daniel realized his hands were clenched and sweaty. He consciously relaxed them.

"You could take a medical discharge with full honors. You've done more than your share for your country. You could settle somewhere permanently with that lovely young family of yours, make a new life doing whatever you'd like."

He thought of his father and how for years Pete had hoped he'd join him in his legal business, but he'd finally given up and retired, accepting that Daniel was not a suit-and-tie kind of guy. There was no opportunity left there.

"Or," said Colonel Small, his eyes brightening, "you might be just the man I've been looking for to spearhead a new project ordered from above."

Daniel shifted his weight in the chair and leaned forward, suddenly catching some of the colonel's enthusiasm.

"I would like you to set up a new department, dedicated to smoothing the process for our wounded soldiers as they transition back to the civilian world. Facilitate them to access training for new work, or to help them go back to school, or to find a network of employers ready to give them a hand up. Whatever would be best for each soldier."

"Would this pertain to those physically wounded, or would soldiers suffering with emotional wounds be included?"

"The parameters would be open to discussion."

He could already think of several directions he would like to take this new assignment, and several old buddies who could help. His mind moved to other soldiers who could have benefited greatly from such a program. He'd need counselors, occupational therapists, career advisors, contacts with local trades programs and colleges...

His thoughts spun with the possibilities, and he needed to force his attention back to what the colonel was saying.

"I don't expect an answer right away. Talk the options over with your wife… Gloria, right? I should have mentioned it right away, but I was sorry to hear about your home. Has she settled into base housing well? Let me know if you need anything to make the transition easier."

Again, Daniel had to slow his racing thoughts to respond. "Thank you, sir. Yes, she's done an amazing job of adjusting to everything that happened. I'm lucky to have such a capable wife. And Lieutenant Meyers should be commended for organizing the risky extraction of our belongings."

He reached across the desk to shake the colonel's hand. "I will talk to Gloria before I give you my answer, sir, but I can tell you right now that your new program sounds like something I would be honored to lead. Its effect could be far-reaching."

The light went out of the colonel's eyes. "So many suicides, Daniel. We have to do something for those who've served our country so that they can hold their heads high as they transition out of the military. But first, go back and work on recuperating." He turned his attention to papers on his desk. "Dismissed."

"Yes, sir," Daniel said, and saluted before turning his chair and wheeling himself out of the office.

He spent the rest of the day having his aide drive him to see each member of his team who had jumped from the plane before him, as well as the wife of the friend he'd lost on the mission. His injury had caused him to miss the memorial service, and he wanted to offer his condolences to her personally.

When he returned home, he was emotionally exhausted and physically depleted, but also anxious to tell Gloria all about their new possibilities. As he expected, she shared his enthusiasm and supported his decision to accept the new assignment.

The morning after Jacquie and Kevin had made love, she rested in the gentle state between sleep and waking, feeling warm and languid and content. She rolled over and Kevin pulled her close. For a moment all was right with the world, and she was where she fit best. Then she came fully awake and remembered her loss. She plummeted back into the almost unbearable grief. Her mother was gone. Her beloved daughter was gone. All sense of safety and faith was gone. She squeezed her eyes shut, held very still and tried to regain the bliss of sleep, but the illusion was over, and her pain would not release her.

She sniffed and Kevin opened his eyes. She watched her husband repeat the same process she'd just experienced. Happiness made him smile at her, but then remembering crushed the contentment and demanded acknowledgement of his pain. His smile faded and his eyes focused far away.

"I dreamed about her," he said, his voice husky with emotion.

"What I'd give to hold her one more time," Jacquie answered.

"At least we have each other to hold again," Kevin said, and they clung to each other, he silently and she with a low moan that gave way to sobs.

When she had quieted, they rose and prepared for work, each deep in their own thoughts. Work was an escape from a house too empty.

The Walters children were asleep, Daniel was in the bathroom getting ready for bed, and Gloria had time, she figured, to check her email.

A new message awaited her, its headline still bolded, from the DNA testing company. Her results were ready! She had opted-in to learn about possible relatives who had also taken the test. After all, that was the whole point: to find family. Might she finally know who her mother was? She clicked into the website immediately.

She skimmed through her nationality percentages quickly. Though interested, she was much more curious about family. Clicking to another page she found that one other client had seemed a very close match, probably a half-sister. Half-sister? Those words flooded her with emotions: disappointment that there wasn't a match that would be her mother; confusion about having a sister; quick jealousy at the thought that maybe her mother kept her half-sister. Anger. Yes, mostly anger. Her mother had abandoned her and then replaced her.

She hit the power button on her computer and the screen went black. She didn't want to know more.

Night Shift

The spring evening was unusually warm, and Miriam walked down the sidewalk carrying a bag with two bottles of lemonade from the convenience store, remembering how much she had enjoyed the lemonade Yosef had shared with her. It was dusk, but she passed several couples who were out for a walk, hand in hand. She stopped in front of a house with a particularly attractive garden.

"Your daffodils are lovely," she called to a woman who rocked on the porch. "And I bet your roses will be breathtaking in June."

"Thank you, they really are at their best then," she answered. "Are you a gardener?"

"I love flowers," Miriam answered. "Do I see hyacinths and tulips in bud, too?"

"Come into the yard. I'll show you around." The woman walked with Miriam around the side of the house, pointing to hydrangeas still leafing out, and rhododendrons with their shiny evergreen leaves. In the backyard she listed what her raised vegetable beds would hold this year, once the ground was warm enough to plant, and what the fruit trees would bear.

On the far side of the house, the woman pointed out what she called her Marian Garden, complete with a statue of Jesus' mother with out-stretched arms. "All the flowers in this garden are mentioned in the Bible, or named for Mary, or symbolic of Mary's life, or figure in stories that have something to do with Mary's life. You can't see them all at this time of year, but there are Rose of Sharon, marigolds, lilies, of course, reminiscent of her purity, and iris whose long blades remind us of the sorrows that pierced Mary's heart. Some people say the lavender bush first grew fragrant flowers when Mary spread Jesus' clothes on them to dry."

"This is truly touching," Miriam said. She ran her fingers over last year's rosemary and awakened its aroma. "It's a beautiful tribute."

As they circled back to the porch, she invited Miriam to sit with her a while.

"I happen to have bought two bottles of lavender lemonade," said Miriam. "I'm new to lemonade, and I've never tasted it flavored with lavender before. Will you try some with me?"

Before long, the women were rocking together on the porch in the dark and deepening their conversation.

"You seem a bit sad," observed Miriam.

"Ah, does it still show?" She took another sip from the bottle. "This is delicious, by the way. Thank you."

Miriam simply nodded and waited.

"I have twin girls who are busy with school functions tonight. They'll both be leaving for college in the fall. Then my nest will be empty." She paused as if deciding before she continued. "You see, I was widowed a few months ago."

She met Miriam's eyes but continued before Miriam could offer her condolences. "My husband had a heart attack, totally unexpected. He was a dentist. I worked in the office as his bookkeeper and receptionist. I received a call at the office from a woman who obviously didn't know I was his wife, telling me 'Dr. Spencer' had collapsed at her house and was on his way in an ambulance to the hospital." She paused. "I don't know why I'm telling a stranger this. I guess I've kept it to myself too long. You have an openness about you that makes me feel safe."

Miriam encouraged her with another nod.

"He was supposed to be at the gym. He scheduled his workout for every Tuesday and Thursday after lunch. I had no idea that was a lie. So, on one very normal day, I lost my husband, my job, our income, and my self-respect."

"You weren't the one who did anything wrong. You have no reason to be ashamed," Miriam said with both reassurance and understanding in her tone. "Do your daughters know?"

The woman sighed. "They loved their daddy so much. I wouldn't take away their admiration for him. No one else knows but the woman on the other end of the phone. Most of the time I'm doing okay. The first shock is over. Now I'm simply dreading September when it feels like my purpose in life will be over, with the girls gone and my marriage and job gone, too. To top it off, today's my birthday. I hit 50."

"A Jubilee Woman!" Miriam said, raising her bottle of lemonade to the woman, as if to toast the happy occasion. "Congratulations. Our Father proclaimed to Leviticus that each 50th year should be one of liberation, forgiveness, rest, and mercy. I hope it is a jubilant year for you. A new start." She grew more serious. "What would your ideal day look like, if you could spend it any way you wanted?"

"That's easy. I'd spend it in a garden. Every day that I spent at the dentist office I wished I were outside planting."

"So why don't you? You certainly have the green thumb. You could look for a gardening job, or if you don't need the money, you could volunteer at one of Portland's beautiful gardens." She ticked off on her fingers: "The Rose Garden, the Rhododendron Garden, the Japanese Garden, or the Chinese Garden."

121

"We do have some beautiful gardens to choose from, don't we? Do you think they'd hire an amateur like me? I suppose I could take some courses, to learn more."

"I can see you as a Master Gardener before long!"

"You know, I could be, couldn't I?"

A quiet enthusiasm in the woman's voice made Miriam smile. She stood then to go, and the woman rose and gave her a warm embrace.

"Thank you! I'm so glad you stopped by and brightened my birthday! Maybe my girls won't be the only ones returning to school this fall!"

CHAPTER 16

Two days later, Jacquie lay in bed trying to prepare herself for the now familiar return of grief that came with morning light. She tried to snuggle closer to Kevin to draw comfort from his presence, but the motion made her stomach lurch. She flew from the bed and barely made it to the toilet where she wretched again and again.

"No!" she yelled when she finally had emptied all that her stomach held. "No, no, no!"

Kevin stumbled into the bathroom, a book from his nightstand raised and ready to attack whatever threatened his wife. He looked confused.

Jacquie, too sick to explain, leaned over the toilet again but only produced dry heaves. "I can't be pregnant!" she groaned. "It's only been a couple days since we made love—" She succumbed to the interruption of a new round of heaving.

"Pregnant?" Kevin repeated, which earned him a death stare from his wife.

"I don't remember morning sickness being this bad before," Jacquie said. "Kevin, I can't do this again. Not yet! It hurts too much to love and lose!"

He helped her back to her bed, brought her a mint to suck on and a bowl, just in case, and then cleaned up the bathroom.

In those moments she loved her husband more than ever before. She tried to ask him to bring crackers to her bedside, but the thought of food made her stomach queasy again and talking would take too much effort. She heard him phoning her boss before she fell back to sleep.

Two days had passed since Gloria had learned she might have a half-sister. She had mulled the idea over whenever her mind wasn't occupied by children or Daniel. She was rehashing her thoughts during breakfast.

"What's up, Gloria," Daniel asked. "You haven't been yourself for a couple of days. Are you worried about something?"

She looked at Daniel and smiled. So sweet of him to notice and be concerned. "I'm thinking about my mother. Trying to decide whether to contact my maybe-half-sister. What do you think I should do?"

"What are you worried about happening?"

It was a good question. How could knowing more about her family hurt her? She was happily married, and if her sister or her mother rejected her, well, she had lived a lifetime of her mother's rejection already. She wouldn't be all alone. She had her own little family now, and a couple of grandparents for her children, too. What was scaring her?

"I guess I'm afraid to know why my mother left me, but still had another daughter. Why wasn't I good enough? What made her get rid of me and try again?"

Daniel wheeled over to her side of the table and reached out. She settled onto his lap and accepted his hug gratefully.

"Maybe the half-sister shared a father with you, not a mother. Or maybe she came first. Maybe your mother abandoned her, too. Maybe you knew her and don't remember."

She hadn't thought of those possibilities, but she doubted there was a sister she simply forgot.

"You won't know if you don't pursue the lead," Daniel said. "You've waited since you were four for a clue like this. Go on. Go email her. I'll watch the kids for a while."

He was right, of course. She didn't need this sister or her mother. She had Daniel and her children, and he would always be there for her, God willing.

She hurried to her laptop and began an email to send through the genetic testing company.

Hi,

She stopped typing. What to say? She started typing again quickly so she wouldn't second guess herself.

> *My name is Gloria Walters. I don't know what my family name was because my mother abandoned me when I was four, and I didn't know my last name, and I never found her.*

Well, that sounded pathetic, but she plunged forward.

> *The genetics company says we might be half-sisters. I've spent 20 years trying to find my mother and learn more about myself. Did you live with her? How old are you? I'm 24. Is she still alive? What was or is her name? Did she talk about me? Did she say why she left me at a hospital and never returned?*

Even more pathetic, she thought, but she continued.

> *If we are related and you know anything, would you be willing to meet? All I want is information, I wouldn't expect anything else from you. Or her.*

Gloria added her direct email address and hit send without reading it over, for fear she would think better of the whole idea and back down. Now she would have to wait to see if there would be an answer. She had become proficient at waiting over all these years. What other choice did she have?

She recalled words Miriam had said to her, "Forgiving is balm to the soul," or something like that.

Where was Miriam? It had been days since she had seen her, and she missed her. She would love to tell her about Daniel being home. Might she ask her whether she had a husband named Yosef that she had sent to look for Daniel? It sounded silly to even think it likely, but something about Miriam was just mysterious enough that anything might be possible.

She wished she had asked Miriam for some way to contact her, though she couldn't quite imagine her friend owning or even using a phone. Where did she live? How did she always show up at just the right time? When the house exploded, she was there. When the soldiers came to tell her Daniel was missing, she was there. She hoped it wouldn't require another disaster to bring her back!

Jacquie heard a gentle knock on her bedroom door and rolled cautiously over in bed to check her clock. She had slept most of the day away. Her head ached. As she tried to sit up, she realized her whole body ached. If this feeling lasted nine months, or even the first trimester, she was sure she wouldn't make it. No way could she eat, feeling like this.

Kevin entered, carrying a cup and saucer. The aroma of mint tea enticed her enough to take a sip. The crackers on the saucer would have to wait. She took a second sip but then flew to the bathroom again, this time feeling weak and dizzy and having to touch walls to keep her balance. She lost the tea and then contended with dry heaves again. She sat on the floor near the toilet, waiting.

"Aw, I'm sorry, hon," Kevin said, but then groaned and lurched toward her. What was he doing?

She knew immediately when he vomited into the sink above her. When he finished, he slid down the bathroom vanity and joined her on the floor. Shivering a little, she rested her hand on his forehead.

"You're burning up."

"I'd make some joke about us both being pregnant, but I don't have the energy to be funny," he said. He started to groan then, and she scooted away from the toilet just in time to give him room to retch again.

"Stomach flu," she said, and realized though she mainly felt relieved, a very small part of her was disappointed.

Night Shift

Miriam knelt down in a large ornate room next to a man so deep in prayer that he didn't notice. Except for red shoes, he was dressed all in white, including a beanie that covered his bowed head and a short cape over his shoulders. After a few moments, she slipped her arm around his back and gave the humble man a side hug. He looked at her then, a huge smile brightening his serious features. "You're back," he said, with the sound of a man rescued on the brink of death.

"I am. Though not for long. I couldn't leave without praying with you before I go."

"Will I be hearing about your visit? Will a new basilica need to be built?" his voice was teasing.

"Not this time. Just small, private interventions."

"Thank you." He stood, and she did as well. He faced her and took her two hands in his. "Thank you for whatever miraculous good you did for our people."

"It is always my pleasure to help my children and your lambs."

"We love you, Mary."

"I love you all more," she teased.

"No doubt, no doubt, for you have carried Love himself!" He knelt again, this time down on one knee like a knight awaiting his lady's favor. He looked up at her. "Mary, pray for me. I want only to please our God, but the way isn't always clear. Pray for our world, that we treat it as the gift God meant it to be. Pray for my lambs, that they may follow your Son, and that my fellow clergy will lead them and love them as He did, as good shepherds."

Miriam drew him up to standing then and embraced him with warmth. She stepped back and met his gaze.

"Amen," she said. "I do and I will. Trust how very much God loves each of his people, and that includes you."

He acknowledged her words with a nod, but then his face crumpled like a child whose beloved mother was leaving. "Come back soon!" he said, and after one more tender smile, she was gone.

CHAPTER 17

When Gloria awoke, she immediately checked her email. Only one was new, but it was what she hoped. She opened it:

Dear Gloria,

Hi, Sis! I've been hoping we would find each other someday.

My name is Angela. And yes, I believe we are half-sisters with the same mother. I guess Mom liked heavenly names.

Gloria sighed, wanting to know more than what names her mother liked. She'd collected so many unanswered questions over the years. But maybe Angela knew some of the answers. She read on, hoping to finally know something more about her mother than she had since she was four. But the rest of the email was short.

I'd love to meet you and tell you all I know. I'd love, love to know you and I'd love, love, love to have a sister! I live in Seattle. Where are you? If you are local, we could meet at noon for lunch on the Quad at University of Washington. I'm six feet two, and a redhead, so you'll have no trouble finding me. I'll bring sandwiches.

That was it. The Quad, at University of Washington, in Seattle. She looked at her watch. Noon was five hours away. But she had children to watch and a husband in a wheelchair, and in morning traffic, Seattle could be a four-hour drive!

She printed out the email and ran to Daniel. He seemed as excited as she was and insisted that she needed to go right away.

"Should we all drive there?" she asked. "But maybe two little ones would overwhelm her. Should I drive alone? I'm so nervous! No, I'm excited, but I'm not sure that I should drive that far in this state of mind."

"I'll call a taxi or rideshare to take you to the airport," Daniel said. He seemed to be in special ops mode, ready to take charge and set things in motion. "You tell her you're coming, then get online and book a flight in a couple hours. It takes less than an hour by air. You can take another ride share to the Quad."

"But the kids, can you handle Winnie and Peter alone?"

He looked down at his wheelchair and took a deep breath. "You'd need to get Peter out of the crib, and maybe I can call around for some help," but his voice reflected his doubt, as well as his disappointment to be unfit for this duty.

"It's okay," said Gloria. "We can schedule something a little further out. Maybe your folks could come with some notice."

Daniel's face mirrored her own disappointment. Then a knock on the door distracted them.

"Miriam!" Winnie squealed as she ran from her bedroom to the door.

"How did she know?" asked both Daniel and Gloria, for Gloria checked the window in the door, and could see Winnie was right.

Still a bit dumbstruck, Gloria opened the door and stepped aside to let Miriam enter.

Winnie wasn't hesitant, though. She threw her arms around Miriam's legs. "I'm so happy to see you, Miriam! Can you stay and play? All day?"

"That's precisely why I am here," Miriam said, and shot Gloria a quick smile. She turned back to Winnie. "I heard your daddy came home, and I thought maybe he and your mama would like a day to themselves while you and Peter and I have a day to ourselves!"

Miriam winked at Gloria, then extended her hand to Daniel, who hadn't found his voice yet, but he shook hands. "Daniel," she said, "What a blessing to see you home and looking well. I'm Miriam."

At this Gloria remembered her manners and spoke up. "Daniel, this is the friend I told you about who rescued us from the house, and who was here with me when I got news of you being missing, and who has a knack for appearing when I need her."

"Um, nice to meet you," Daniel managed. Then, snapping back to himself he said, "Welcome. You are always welcome in our home. I can't tell you how much I appreciate your help. Thank God you were there when the explosion happened."

"Amen!" Miriam answered.

Miriam sent Winnie for one of Henry's loaned books to read, and that gave Gloria time to explain about her email. "We were just considering flying to Seattle." She turned to Daniel, "Can we afford that?"

"We can, but I don't want to slow you down. Why don't you go, and Miriam and I will hold down the fort, if that's okay with her?"

It seemed like a good solution to Gloria, though she might have felt more confident meeting her sister if Daniel were with her. Yet, she also liked the idea of Daniel getting to know Miriam. She would have loved to spend a whole day with Miriam herself. The gentle woman radiated happiness. No, more than happiness, she emanated a deep, peaceful joy.

At 11:00, Gloria's plane touched down. She had no luggage, so climbed into a ride share within 15 minutes. At precisely noon, she stepped onto the University of Washington Quad. The sight took her breath away.

Cherry trees at the peak of their blossoming surrounded the grassy rectangle and their aroma filled the air. Walkways crisscrossed the green lawn and students hurried like ants along them. In the center stood one young woman who was tall, and crowned with long, dark red hair that the sun made shine like a polished chestnut. Gloria walked to her and asked, "Angela?"

"You must be Gloria!" Angela enveloped her with a long embrace, then stepped back. "You have our mom's eyes and hair."

Gloria could have hugged her sister again for sharing a bit of such longed-for information.

"Come," said Angela, and she steered them through the ant-parade of students to a wooden bench under the trees. From her backpack, she handed Gloria a brown bag packed with a turkey sandwich, an apple, and a pint carton of chocolate milk. Angela opened her own bag and started eating, but around a mouthful of food said, "Fire away! Ask me whatever you'd like to know." Then she continued to chew.

Gloria was too excited to eat, and her questions volleyed like when her husband used to take her to shooting practice. "What's Mom's name? Is she here in Seattle? Do you live with her? Does she talk about me? Are there other siblings? Did you know your father? Did you know mine?" She left unasked the most important question: Why did she leave me?

By the time she paused for a breath, Angela had finished her sandwich and began to answer.

"My—I mean our—mother's name is Didi Cruz. She didn't abandon me the way she did you. She placed me in an open adoption, so I grew up knowing her. She told me about you just a few days ago, and says she never completely forgave herself for leaving you at the hospital.

"You see," continued Angela, "Didi—that's what I called her because my adoptive mother feels like my real mom—had severe bipolar disorder."

"I've wondered about that. I remember her sometimes being great fun and other times not leaving her bed for days."

"Do you remember burning yourself?"

"Yes." How could she forget? That was the day her mother left her.

"I guess that day made her decide she wasn't fit to take care of you, to be a good mom. She had been awake when you tried to cook yourself some lunch, and she knew she should get up and cook for you, but she didn't have the energy. Then when you burned yourself, she felt horrible. She decided you wouldn't be safe living with her. And she couldn't face the doctors and tell them how the accident happened, so she dropped you off and drove to a different hospital where she checked herself in for treatment."

"Did she improve with treatment? Wouldn't she have come and found me if she got better?"

"I guess she improved but didn't manage to stay stable. She'd feel better balanced on the medicine, and then think she didn't need it anymore, so she'd stop taking it. Then she'd spiral down or out of control until she would check herself back into a hospital."

From what Angela was saying, Gloria got the idea she was preparing her for bad news. Was her mother dead? No, she said Didi had just talked to her about Gloria days ago.

"When she was manic," Angela continued, "she went a bit wild, if you know what I mean, so that's how I came to be, about a year after she left you. She knew right away that she couldn't keep me, she said, so she arranged an open adoption. I have great parents, and I grew up knowing Didi, too." She laid her hand over Gloria's. "I'm sorry you didn't get to."

Both young women were silent then for a while.

It seemed there was something Angela was trying not to say, and Gloria didn't want to push too hard. "Do you have a photo of her?" Gloria asked.

"Oh, yes, I forgot!" Angela rummaged through her backpack. "I printed these out for you."

Gloria saw a woman with a wide smile, though her dark eyes had a worried look to them. She had dark hair, but beyond that, Gloria couldn't see the resemblance that Angela had. She wished the woman in the photo seemed familiar but her four-year-old memories had long since lost their sharpness. Still, she would be happy to keep these photos. She could show her children what their grandma looked like, and there was some consolation in that.

"Did she ever say anything about my father?" Gloria hadn't pursued finding out about him. Though there was little to go on to find her mother, there was absolutely nothing she knew about her father.

"No," said Angela softly, "nor mine. I suspect they were both one-night flings during a manic phase, though mine must have been tall and redheaded and hard to forget!" She giggled and Gloria admired how easily laughter came to this new sister of hers.

Angela grew serious again. "That's part of why I did the DNA testing. I'd like to know about him ...I think."

They both bit into their apples and chewed a while before Gloria worked up enough courage to ask, "You talk about her in past tense. Why?"

Angela paused, looked directly at Gloria as if sizing her up, then seemed to decide. She took a deep breath.

"Didi started self-medicating with alcohol and drugs and was often homeless. She wouldn't accept any help when my parents and I tried. Eventually her erratic life took its toll. Someone found her collapsed in a homeless camp and took her to the hospital. From there she was sent to a kind of rehab/nursing home."

"And?" That was all Gloria could ask, though she really didn't want to hear the answer.

Angela took a deep breath. "I wanted to meet you, to be sure you weren't bitter and angry before I decided whether to take you to her. She's dying. I didn't want you to upset her."

She had found her mother almost too late to meet her.

In the military apartment, Miriam and Daniel made a good team taking care of the children. They walked to the nearby playground and discovered that Winnie could make Peter giggle by running circles around his stroller. Miriam had brought Peter's bear blanket and spread it on the ground so he could wiggle and stretch and enjoy the beautiful spring air. Daniel pushed Winnie on the swings and coached her in learning to pump, but when she lost interest and joined others in the sandbox, he rolled himself over to the blanket Miriam shared with Peter and parked the wheelchair alongside.

"Beautiful day," she said. "What a blessing."

"For a while there, I didn't think I'd ever see another beautiful spring day."

"Gloria never gave up hope."

"Neither did I really, at least once Yosef found me." He watched her face to see if she would show any recognition.

She simply smiled and said, "God was very good to you."

"He was, indeed." But he couldn't leave it at that. "Miriam, you've shown up repeatedly, precisely when my family needed you. And Yosef arrived right when I needed him most, too, saying a Miriam sent him to me. Are you that Miriam?"

She smiled and looked at him—deep into his soul, he felt—and repeated, "God was very good to you." Then she stood abruptly. "Let's go make a feast for Gloria's return!"

Daniel remembered a Bible verse his mother used to quote: "Do not neglect to show hospitality to strangers, for by doing that some have entertained angels without knowing it." He hadn't shown Miriam hospitality, in fact, she had been the one to bless them with her help, but might she be other-worldly?

Gloria and Angela shared a ride to their mother's nursing home. Sitting together in the back seat, but in earshot of the driver, led them to chat about less emotional things.

Gloria realized that she needed to alter her dream of a future with her mother and be grateful to have found this sister. They should begin to build a relationship. "What are you studying?" she asked.

"I'm still deciding. I'm a first-year student, and I'm taking general studies courses. There are so many wonderful options, I hate to focus in on a major too soon."

"What do you love to do?" Gloria wondered what she might have chosen to study, if she had the chance to attend college. At Angela's age, she was supporting herself at the diner, not selecting whatever classes she'd like to pursue. Still, she wasn't jealous. If not for the diner, she wouldn't have met Daniel.

"I'm an artist at heart." Angela said. "I love to sing and paint and write poetry, none of which will support me reliably. So, I'm considering a business degree. Or maybe teaching. I love kids, too!"

Then Gloria told Angela about her children, showed her their photos on her phone, and talked about Daniel and how she almost lost him only days ago.

"Wow, you've done a lot for only being five years older than I am! I better get a move on!"

"Is there a special someone in your life? Are you dating?"

Angela had a wide circle of friends, she said, though no one particular soulmate. They talked more freely now, leaving behind the awkwardness of just meeting. But as they drove up to the nursing home, both sank into the silence of their own thoughts.

Angela led Gloria to a gently lit room, and to the bedside of a woman asleep. Angela leaned over the bed and kissed the woman's cheek. "Didi," she said, "I found Gloria. She's here."

Gloria watched her mother's eyes open wide as she turned toward her. Something did seem familiar about her face and the realization brought such a mix of emotions that the woman's features blurred through Gloria's tears.

"Gloria?" her mother's voice was weak but hopeful. She reached toward her.

Gloria took her mother's hand. "Mama? Is it really you? I've looked for you for so long." She didn't mean to sound accusatory, so she softened her voice. "I'm so happy to find you!"

Tears gathered in her mother's eyes. "I'm sorry," she said, but her words started a cough. When she caught her breath, she continued. "Forgive me? Please?"

"Angela told me that you were trying to do what was best for me. I had thought you were angry about the fire." There, she had admitted her worst fears about that day, that her mother left her because of what she did. Or maybe because she wasn't good enough.

"Angry at myself.... Only myself." Didi coughed again. "I always loved you.... Every day since you were born.... I ached to hold you again, to be able to explain." The next cough took away her voice. She whispered, "So ashamed of myself."

Then, what Gloria had always hoped, happened. She let go of her past and forgave herself and her mother. She leaned over the bed and wrapped her arms around her mother, surprised at how bony and thin the woman felt. She released Didi and through her tears she said, "I love you, Mama. I understand now."

In that moment she knew what Miriam had said was true. Forgiveness held a balm. Her healing had begun.

Didi reached a hand to each of her daughters. "I never stopped... loving you both," she said. Then, as if she had stayed alive simply for this reunion, she slipped away.

"I wish I could stay," Gloria said to Angela later, before climbing into her ride to the airport.

"I'm relieved that you got to see our mother before it was too late. Bringing you meant I was there, too, when she died. It seemed like a little miracle."

I've been blessed by a few miracles lately, Gloria thought, but only said, "Something else to be grateful for."

"My mom and dad have offered to pay for the burial," Angela said. "They've always declared she gave them the greatest gift when she shared me with them." She blushed a little. "They're happy to do it. I don't think we will do a funeral, but maybe when you can come back, we can do a quiet, private memorial service."

"I'll definitely come back soon for a memorial, and I'll bring my family. I'll look forward to meeting your parents."

With that and a final hug, Gloria climbed into the backseat of the waiting ride share car.

Emotionally exhausted, she was anxious to return home. She had quite a story to tell Daniel and Winnie. She wondered how they were getting along with Miriam. Once she was buckled into her seat on the airplane and before closing her eyes for a rest, she reminded herself to finally get some contact information from that mysterious friend.

At 6:00 pm, Gloria was met by a very excited Winnie at the apartment door. The aroma in her little kitchen made her stomach growl. The table was set, complete with a bouquet of dandelions in the center. She lifted the lid of a large pot on the stove and was rewarded with treats for her nose and eyes. The pot was simmering with diced chicken, corn, carrots, onions, and barley. On the counter next to the stove was a lovely homemade loaf of brown bread.

Daniel rolled in from the living room with his knees holding Peter on his lap and his hands pushing the large wheels of his chair. After a hug, he asked if she had run into Miriam on her way into the apartment. "She left just seconds ago," he said.

"No," Gloria answered and tried to hide her disappointment. "I didn't see her, but I'm so happy to see you three!" She had hoped to learn more about Miriam, to share a meal and a good long talk. She had, however, been able to do that with her sister, so after serving the soup, the little family sat together and caught up on their day apart.

"So, what did you do with Miriam?" she asked after telling them about Angela. She would wait to tell Daniel about her mother when they were alone.

"We went to the playground!" sang Winnie, and then added in an off-key melody, "Miriam sang us lots of songs. I like to sing like her now."

Peter laughed from his highchair.

"Giggles from Peter!" Gloria had missed his first laugh that morning but was delighted to hear him now.

"We spent a while at the playground," Daniel agreed, "and I tried to ask about Yosef, but your Miriam can be evasive when she wants to be. I can't figure her out."

"Did you talk more when you came back here? There must have been quiet time during the kids' naps."

Daniel looked sheepish. "She suggested I lie down for a few minutes while the children rested and I did, fully intending to get up soon, but I slept deeply until Winnie woke up. By then Miriam was putting finishing touches on the dinner, and Peter needed attention, and before we knew it, she took her leave."

"The mystery woman stays a mystery," Gloria said with a sigh. And she still had no idea how to contact her.

Jacquie and Kevin had spent the rest of the day in bed, alternating between trying very hard not to move and flying out of bed for the bathroom. It was all they could do to make it there and back. In the late evening, they both ignored a noise they heard on their front porch. Whatever was there could wait until tomorrow. Or next year, by the way they felt.

Night Shift

Martha was a bit confused. Feeling muddled struck more and more often, but it certainly seemed that her favorite statue of Mary had climbed down off its shelf and was now sitting with her on her bed.

"What are you looking at?" Asked Miriam, pointing to papers in Martha's hands.

"Results from a memory test I took," Martha answered. "My children arranged it. They are arranging a lot of things lately."

"They love you and worry about you. What do the results say?"

"Moderate dementia." Martha shrugged. "I suppose it's true. Lately I show up for things either at the wrong time or on the wrong day. I can't remember all my grandchildren's names, let alone the great-grandchildren. My daughter says I have four great-great grandchildren, but that can't be true. I'm not that old."

"What a blessing to see your family grow!" Miriam said to the elderly woman. "One of the wishes in the Bible is to see your children's children. Very few get to live long enough to see as many generations as you."

"But now it seems I am outliving my mind. Losing important memories. And I suppose it will only get worse." Martha set down the paper and removed her reading glasses. "Who am I, if not a collection of the memories of my life? Who will remember my story when I can't?"

"The diseases of this life that slowly take away a person's memories are certainly a sorrow. But you know the Father can turn even this to good."

"What good can it possibly be to slowly stop knowing all I worked so many years to learn? What worth is there in the remainder of a life like that?"

"Martha," Miriam said softly, "isn't a newborn's life a precious treasure, even though he or she holds no memories?"

Martha scowled, suspecting where this line of thought was going, so Miriam continued. "A child can teach a parent to discover what it is to love, unconditionally, that little bundle of demands, even though the newborn gives nothing in return, not even a smile until it is older."

The statue-now-woman looked intently into Martha's eyes. "We don't understand all God's ways, or how he works all things for good, even devastating things like this, but perhaps he is giving your family and friends and caretakers a gift by allowing them to serve you."

"I don't want to be a burden to anyone! I want to continue to be useful, to help people!" Martha would have stomped her foot if she hadn't been sitting on her bed.

"And bless you for that desire. But believe me, as difficult as the time ahead may be for everyone, eventually your family will look back and count your final days with them as a blessing. Yes, they will be sad if you reach a point when you don't know who they are anymore, but they will know you! They will carry the memories of you as precious gifts. And have faith; you will rise whole and healthy again in the next life. This suffering is temporary, and your reward will be immeasurable and permanent!"

Martha sighed. "Aging seems to be a tiresome series of letting go, one thing after another. I miss my own home, and yes, I'm grateful, of course, that my daughter has taken me into her home, but I miss my healthy, flexible body. I miss being able to eat whatever I wanted before I had to start watching my salt intake, my cholesterol levels, or my blood sugar. I miss driving! Must I really let go of my memories, too?"

"Only God knows what lies ahead, but I promise you, He is good: all loving, all merciful, all wise. He will be with you."

Martha nodded. Yes, there was comfort in that, knowing He would be with her, even if she no longer knew Him. She bowed her head and her will and did what she had done many times before. She placed herself in His hands and her life at His disposal. With that came peace.

When she looked up again, she laughed to see her Mary statue back on the shelf, with the same serene face she always wore. Had her statue truly climbed down and joined her on her bed? Maybe it didn't matter. Her future might not always allow her to tell what was real and what wasn't, but Martha knew that tonight's message touched her heart with profound truth.

CHAPTER 18

In the morning, when Jacquie hadn't heaved for a few hours and thought she had regained a little strength, she put on her robe and went to the front door, hoping their newspaper wasn't very far down the driveway. There on her porch was a cooler with ice inside, and a large container of chicken soup with a note that said, "For when you feel better. Love, Miriam."

Jacquie rolled her eyes. She wondered which Miriam this was, and then wondered why it mattered.

Checking email mid-morning, Gloria answered a sweet message from Angela saying how much she had enjoyed her visit and asking when a good day for a memorial would be. Gloria checked the calendar on her phone to figure out when she and her little family could attend. The app reminded her she was due to visit Henry Martin's house today for their classes and was already late. She enjoyed her time with Henry and had made strides in her reading, just as he had become more adept with cooking. When she called and checked to see if it would still work, Henry invited her to come soon and enjoy a lunch he was making. He asked her to bring Daniel, as well.

Daniel said he felt a bit stir-crazy and was happy for a reason to leave the base. "I never realized you had trouble with reading," he said as they got themselves and the kids ready.

"I worked pretty hard to hide it. Then while you were gone, I visited with some of the wives here. I checked on the room where the children had congregated and saw our Winnie sitting next to one of the older girls who was reading stories to the little ones. She looked so happy and focused. It made me realize I don't read to her. I never even thought to have books for her in the house.

"Miriam had suggested I go see Henry, a friend of hers, who happens to be retired and used to be a reading specialist." She chuckled. "And a very bad cook. So, we trade classes. He's recently lost his wife," she explained. "I know you'll like him. I'm glad he invited you along."

"I like his house," Winnie piped up. "He has toys and is always nice to me. I wish he had kids, though, to play with."

When Winnie had run to her room to gather his books in hopes of borrowing new ones, Gloria added, "Henry lost a little grandchild lately. His first, I think. He and his wife had prepared a room full of toys and books for the little one before his wife died of cancer."

"The poor guy," said Daniel. "He's lost a lot in a very little time, and I bet he gets lonely."

"Kind of puts losing our house into perspective."

"We've got our family," agreed Daniel. "Everything else is a bonus, but not critical."

"Thank God you came back to us, my love." Gloria bent and kissed him. She wasn't accustomed to the chair making spontaneous hugs more difficult, but it was temporary. Daniel would walk again. More bonus. Thanks to the mysterious Yosef.

And Miriam? Deep down, Gloria felt Miriam had something to do with her husband's safety. The whole family was indebted to her and yet, what could they do for a friend who wouldn't tell them much about herself, even where she lived?

At Henry's house, Gloria unbuckled Winnie first, who very seriously gathered the three books and walked ceremoniously to the house. Gloria rolled the wheelchair to Daniel's open car door and set the brakes. He could manage the rest. Next, she unbuckled and lifted

Peter into her arms. She slung the diaper bag over her shoulder and arrived at the door just as Henry opened it.

"Mr. Martin," Winnie said very soberly, "I took good care of your books and kept Peter from hurting them. May I trade these for some new ones?"

Henry knelt to her level and inspected the books carefully. "Winnie, you've done a great job being careful. Yes, you may run to the playroom and choose five this time!"

"You are so sweet to her, Henry," said Gloria. "Thank you." She motioned toward her husband. "This is Daniel, home safe and sound."

"Or will be sound, soon," Daniel said. "Pleased to meet you, Henry." The two men shook hands before Henry led them into his kitchen.

"Smells wonderful!" said Gloria. "What are you making?"

"Chicken and vegetable soup from scratch!" he answered proudly.

"You've moved up since boxed macaroni and cheese," she teased.

"I have to keep up with the progress you're making on reading," Henry said, and then looked to Gloria with wide eyes. "I'm sorry if I've spilled the beans."

"No, no," said Daniel, "Gloria is proud of the work you two have done together. I'm proud of her, too. And I appreciate you helping her."

With that, both men seemed to relax, and Gloria happily settled the children at the table Henry had set. She cooled the soup for Winnie and separated some egg noodles and soft carrot bits out for Peter to play with on the highchair tray.

She had been right, the men did seem to immediately like each other and before long were talking about work, as men usually did in her experience.

"What do you do for the military?" Henry asked.

Daniel told him about the new challenge he'd taken on, helping soldiers to transition from the military to civilian life again.

Gloria loved listening to him talk about his work. Always before, he could only give her the barest of information about what he did. Now he talked at length about the different ways he could see this assignment developing.

"What kind of help do you need most?" Henry asked.

"Well, one thing I'm feeling inadequate about is helping the men who are ready to find new work be introduced into the business world.

I've found a good system of references for medical care and have contacted the local colleges about continuing education, so I have a good start in those areas."

Henry nodded, seeming deep in thought.

Gloria used the pause in conversation to compliment her student. "Henry, this soup is delicious!" She had come across a few little bones she'd pushed to the side of her bowl, but for a first effort, he'd done an amazing job.

"I've graduated to reading recipes and giving them a shot," he said. "I'm enjoying it but cooking for one isn't nearly as much fun as having guests over. At least guests that are very understanding," he said, as he lifted a rather large bone out of his bowl. "Wasn't quite sure how to hide this," he said, showing them the bone and laughing.

Winnie asked to be excused, then carefully carried her bowl with two hands over to the kitchen counter near the dishwasher. After her mother checked to be sure her hands were clean, she disappeared into the toy room.

"Daniel," Henry said, serious again, "I've been looking for ways to feel useful, and if you'll have me, I'd love to volunteer my services being a liaison with the business world."

"But aren't you a reading specialist?" asked Daniel.

"I only stayed with that career for a few years," Henry answered. "For the next 35 years, I was quite a businessperson, if I do say so myself. I built up a company with many tutors, eventually adding online services and college counseling. I even led the Chamber of Commerce for a while. I've got the kind of connections your soldiers will need."

By the look on Daniel's face, Gloria was very glad she took Miriam's advice weeks ago and looked up her friend Henry. Another bonus— or blessing—for her whole family.

As the men continued to talk, Gloria lifted a very sleepy Peter from his highchair and wandered to the toy room to check on Winnie. She nursed Peter for a short time and then laid him, fast asleep, in the porta-crib Henry had bought for his granddaughter. Above the crib was a portrait she hadn't seen before. She was startled to recognize Jacquie, her reporter friend, seated and holding a lovely, bright-eyed baby in a pink ruffled dress. In a chair next to her leaned a frail looking woman, who smiled brightly. She must be Henry's wife, and Jacquie's mother, Gloria realized. Behind the chairs stood a proud Henry, and the man who must be Jacquie's husband.

"You've found our family portrait," Henry said behind her.

Gloria turned to him. "It's lovely. Happier times, I know. Is it hard for you to see it?"

"I only yesterday hung it again. For a while I couldn't handle how much it made me miss my beloved wife and sweet grandchild. It reminded me of all we've lost. But since Miriam has come to visit me, now it reminds me of my blessings."

"I didn't realize that I know your daughter," Gloria said.

Daniel had joined them now, too. "It's Jacquie, the reporter who came to our house to interview me."

"And she had interviewed me after our house was destroyed," Gloria added.

"Small world!" Henry said. "Although when Miriam is involved, it feels like everyone is family."

"Has Jacquie met Miriam?" Gloria asked.

"Only briefly, and she didn't realize who Miriam is," he answered, and looked at Gloria questioningly.

Gloria didn't know quite how to respond, but said quietly, "I'm not sure anyone really knows."

Henry chuckled and then offered to read to Winnie, adding, "Next it's your turn, Gloria. Let's see how my star pupil is improving."

"Not as well as mine is," she said. "Your lunch was impressive."

Gloria was ready to turn out the lights in their snug little apartment. The children had been asleep for a couple hours, and now Daniel was lifting himself into the bed.

A light knock at the door made Gloria walk to the door and peek through the curtained window. There stood Miriam!

Gloria opened the door but couldn't figure why anyone would visit at 11:00 p.m.

Before she had said hello, Miriam asked, "May I borrow your car, quickly?"

Gloria lifted the keys off their hook nearby and handed them to her friend. She would do anything for Miriam.

"Thank you, I'll bring it back before morning," she said and hurried away.

Gloria watched her go until she'd turned a corner, then listened as she heard her car start and drive away. "How strange!"

"What's up, honey?" she heard Daniel call.

She closed the door, turned out the kitchen light, and headed to bed. She explained what little she could about the odd interaction, hoping Daniel wouldn't mind her giving their keys away.

"Of course not," he answered. "We should do anything for her after all she's done for us. Though, I guess I'm a little amazed she can drive. She just seems a bit "old world" for that."

"Well, she never ceases to surprise me, that's for sure," said Gloria.

Night Shift

In a different part of town, Miriam parked the little minivan in front of a house, just as a young woman fled out its door, carrying a baby about Peter's size. An angry man was not far behind the woman, raising a crowbar and screaming, "You get back here, or I swear I'll kill you both!"

Miriam reached across the seat and opened the passenger's door and called, "Tiana, jump in!"

Tiana did, slammed the car door behind her, and Miriam sped away, leaving an irate man screaming in the street. He threw the crowbar like a javelin, but it missed its target.

After several turns, and when both women were sure they weren't followed, Miriam parked long enough for Tiana to strap her daughter into Peter's car seat in the back. As soon as she was back in the minivan, Miriam began driving again.

Tiana said, "I'm relieved to put as much distance between me and that man as we can." Then she really looked at Miriam. "Who are you? I thought you were my mother. Your voice sounded just like hers, or I might not have jumped into your car. How did you know I needed you right then?"

Miriam, with skin darker than Tiana's and dressed like older women from the islands, smiled a bright white smile. "Child, my name is Miriam, and I guess I was in the right place at the right time, praise God. Was that your husband?"

"Well, he's my daughter's father. He's not that bad most of the time." She sounded defensive and then softened her voice. "And I love him."

"Mmm hmm," Miriam said, and her tone spoke volumes.

"I do, God help me, I do," said Tiana.

"Love is one thing, and safety is another," said Miriam. "Men can forfeit the right to be with their families by hurting women or children. Your little Jayda, there, depends on you to keep her safe."

"I'd never let him hurt her!"

"You wouldn't mean to, but his anger seems unpredictable and out of control."

"Usually I can see it coming, but not always," she admitted. "Sometimes it isn't me he's angry with at all, but I'm the one who's available."

"Tiana, you would give your life for this baby, am I right?"

Tiana turned to check on her daughter in the backseat. "Absolutely."

"Then for now, you need to sacrifice your feelings for her daddy, and protect her. He's wounded and you can't fix him, but it's possible that losing you two might be just what he needs to make him get help. Promise me you won't go back to him until someone professional assures you he's done the work and can control his temper. Will you promise me that?"

"But where will I go in the meantime?"

Miriam pulled the minivan in front of an ordinary looking, but large house and parked. "Promise me?"

Tiana looked back at her baby, who was now sweetly snoring in the car seat. "Yes, ma'am. I promise."

This is a safe house. They are expecting you and will help you both along the way."

"But…" Tiana shook her head in confusion. "How did you know?"

"Your mama's been talking to me, child. Now scoot! Off you go."

Tiana climbed out of the car, lifted Jayda out of the car seat, and hesitated before closing the door.

"Know you are very, very loved," said Miriam.

"Thank you," said Tiana with a nod. Then she closed the door with a quiet click, straightened her back, and walked up to the door. Before she even knocked, it swung open to her future.

CHAPTER 19

Gloria heard Peter cry just before dawn and rose to nurse him, hoping he'd go back to sleep. As she was returning to her room, a light tapping noise stopped her. She peeked through the curtain at the door and smiled to see Miriam. She let her in, and Miriam whispered as she returned the keys, "Thank you for your car. Two of my children are safe because of it."

"After all you've done for us, I'm delighted to help you in any way I can," Gloria responded, also in a soft voice. She wondered how her car had saved Miriam's children, but it didn't seem right to ask, since Miriam hadn't ever talked about her family. Instead she offered, "Can you come in and visit? I was just thinking of making myself some warm milk to help get back to sleep."

To her surprise, Miriam nodded and followed her into the kitchen. There they could talk more freely, as it was further from the bedrooms.

"Miriam, I'd like to get to know you better. How can I reach you? Maybe you could come have dinner with us soon." She poured two cups of milk, and heated them in the microwave, stopping it before it dinged.

"Gloria, you are gifted with hospitality. I would love to spend more time with you, but I'm afraid I have come to say goodbye. I'll be returning home soon. I've nearly finished what I came here to do."

Gloria set the cups and a container of chocolate powder down on the table and joined her friend, surprised at how disappointed she felt. Though she had spent relatively little time with Miriam, their experiences together had felt momentous, each time filled with difficult emotions due to the circumstances, but also with deep gratitude to Miriam for her gentle assistance.

"Saying I'll miss you seems inadequate. I've come to love you Miriam, like a sister, or dear aunt." She shook her head. "No. Like the mother I spent my childhood wanting."

"I'm so glad you were able to meet your birth mother before she passed away. I'm also very sorry that you didn't have a childhood with her. You must feel her loss deeply, even though she was absent for so long."

How did Miriam know her mother had died? Gloria pushed the question aside. Miriam was like that. She knew things. Big things. That thought brought another question to mind.

"Miriam, what is this life supposed to be really about? I know you've said love and relationship, and I love my husband and family. What deeper am I supposed to be doing?"

Miriam smiled at her and she felt cherished. "My deepest desire for you, is that you come to love God, whether you see Him as Father, Son, or Spirit."

"So, you mean, read the Bible?"

"Yes, read His story and the story of His people, and read what good people write about Him, but do more than that. Talk to Him."

"Say my prayers?

"Yes, but again, more than that. Talk to Him. Talk to Him like you talk to the people you love. Like you are talking to me right now. Share your thoughts. Ask Him questions. Tell Him your worries. Thank Him for the gifts you recognize in your life. Praise Him."

"What does 'praise Him' really mean? Does He need me to tell Him that He's great?"

"All relationships thrive when we acknowledge to each other what is good in what we do. We encourage a friend to be the best they can be. We compliment our children when they make good choices. We thank our parents for all that they've done for us, and for the effort they made to raise us well. We even need to say to ourselves, 'Well done, good job! I knew I could do it if I set my mind to it.'"

"So, praise is like complimenting God on a job well done?"

"In some respects, yes. If you see a beautiful sunset or flower or child, praise and thank God for creating it. But go beyond being grateful for the pleasure that His creation gives your senses. Praise Him because He is all good, even when you don't understand something about His plan. Glorify Him!"

"Glorify? Is that another word for praise?"

"It is. It's acknowledging that He is all Love! Even though evil and pain exist in this world, trust that they aren't from Him, and that He wants to protect you from them."

"I think everyone has trouble with the pain part. If God is all-powerful, how can He choose to allow pain and let innocent ones suffer?"

"Just like we need to trust our friends for our relationships to be strong, God asks us to trust Him. Believe that He is all good, all loving, all merciful. Trust Him that, even when we can't understand, He will triumph over evil. He always does. Sometimes we witness the victory. Sometimes we won't in this life, but always He wins. Always. Love prevails."

"So, talk to Him."

"Yes. Spend time with Him, regularly. All relationships become stronger when we spend time with each other, without any specific agenda, simply to enjoy being together."

After a pause to process Miriam's words, Gloria admitted, "Losing you feels like I've lost two mothers in one week."

"Gloria," Miriam said as she laid her hand over Gloria's. "I love you dearly. Love never ends. And God loves you in depths unimaginable. He watched over you as a child, and He continues to love and watch over you now. He brought Daniel into your diner."

"And out of the desert," Gloria realized.

"And out of the desert," Miriam agreed.

The two women drank their warm milk, neither choosing to make it into cocoa. Gloria didn't ask Miriam to call or write. She sensed she wouldn't hear from Miriam again, but took comfort in the gentle woman's words. Somehow, hearing God sent Daniel to Gloria made her realize her heavenly Father had been with her all along, loving and guiding her, even when she thought she had no family. She believed now that He would continue to do so.

Miriam stood then and reached into a pocket that hadn't been obvious in the tunic she wore. She drew out three intricately and exquisitely carved animals, the size of her palm, made from an especially beautiful wood: a donkey and two lambs.

"They are olive wood, from my homeland. My husband carved

them after Daniel told him about your children. The donkey is for Winnie, and a little bit for Daniel, too. Ask him to keep telling his children about his ride on the donkey. People should always share the stories of the times God intervenes for them. We need to carry these miracles and ponder them in our hearts, but also use them to encourage others."

So, her husband *was* that Yosef.

"One lamb is for you and Peter, so you remember you are always cherished by the Good Shepherd. The other I'll ask you to give to your friend Jacquie when you visit her at the hospital, to give to her next baby."

Gloria took a closer look at the animals, impressed with how beautiful they were. When she glanced back up, she was alone in her kitchen. "Miriam?" But there was no answer. She checked her phone and confirmed her new suspicion. Yes, Miriam and Yosef were Hebrew versions of Mary and Joseph. She suddenly felt immensely treasured. Someone so wonderful had come to help someone so... so her!

She returned to bed, snuggling up to Daniel to enjoy his warmth. She drifted off to sleep quickly. In a dream, Gloria was attending a church memorial service for her mother. Daniel and the children weren't with her, for some reason, and she felt quite alone sitting behind Angela and her adoptive parents. Then Miriam slipped into her pew to sit beside her and hold her hand. At the end of the service Miriam whispered, "You'll see her again, and she will be completely well and completely able to love you as you deserve." When Gloria woke, she knew she would carry that comfort with her at the real memorial service, and whenever the old feelings of abandonment returned. The dream—and Miriam—had brought her the gift of healing.

Jacquie and Kevin were both feeling better that day. Jacquie had made it to work and was starting to recover almost to her old self again. Kevin had decided to stay in bed one more day, which made sense since he'd gotten the flu a day after she had. When she returned home, she found him watching television in his robe on the couch. She plopped down next to him and tried to think what sounded good for dinner. They had almost finished Miriam's soup, and though it was delicious, the mystery of the woman—or women, she reminded herself — kept her from enjoying it fully.

Jacquie couldn't believe it when Kevin started tracing light circles on her thigh. How did the man have energy for what that meant?

"Want to go upstairs?" he asked, wiggling his eyebrows like Charlie Chaplain.

She definitely did not want to go upstairs. The image of both of them hurling into the toilet was still a little too fresh. And the longer since she'd stopped nursing, the better chance of getting pregnant again. No way was she ready for that. Might not ever be. Probably won't ever be, she corrected herself. She couldn't risk that kind of grief again.

Kevin must have read her thoughts. "Jacquie, we need to get back to normal. Maybe trying for another baby would be exactly what we need."

"How many times do I have to tell you I'm not ready! I might not ever be ready! I can't imagine replacing our Rosette!"

The phone rang and cut off what Kevin was about to answer.

"Hi Daddy," she said with a brighter voice than she felt.

Kevin sighed.

"Hi, Hon," said Henry. "I have some great soup here that I made yesterday. Do you and Kevin want to come over for dinner and help me eat it?"

"Dinner? Sounds great, Dad," she answered, wondering why everybody suddenly was making soup. But, looking at Kevin, she appreciated an excuse to leave.

Kevin shook his head no, though he had only heard her side of the conversation. He scowled.

"It will only be me, though. Kevin isn't feeling up to... much yet."

When she had hung up, he grumbled. "You're really going to leave me again? You were gone all day. I miss you, and we need to work this out!"

"I'll heat you up some of Miriam's soup. My Dad has never made soup before, so I didn't want to disappoint him. Besides, I bet you won't last long before you're asleep again."

"Fine," he answered, "but don't stay away too late. A little cuddling would help get me ready for bed."

With any luck you'll be asleep by the time I get back, she thought, and then she popped Miriam's soup into the microwave before she headed out the door. And I'm sure not going to wake you up, if so.

When Jacquie arrived at Henry's house, she could smell freshly baked bread. "Daddy, you're really impressing me. Did you bake the bread, as well as make the soup, or is this your Miriam's doing?"

"I did it all, but in a way it's Miriam's doing, too, because she arranged for me to take cooking classes. And my teacher, it turns out, is someone you know. Gloria Walters."

"Gloria? The woman whose house collapsed, and whose husband disappeared on a mission? How in the world did you two meet up?"

"Miriam suggested she come ask me for some reading help in exchange for cooking classes. I thoroughly enjoy her visits twice a week. She brings her children, too, and they love the playroom we set up."

So, Explosion Miriam and her father's Housekeeper Miriam were the same person. She wanted to be alone to think a moment, so Jacquie walked into the playroom. This had been her parents' project, once they learned she was expecting. It was supposed to be Rosette's room, not for Gloria's children. Not that she resented them using it; she just wished things were different. Turning to take the whole room in, she covered her mouth and blinked quickly when she saw the family portrait. "I thought you put that away," she called.

Henry joined her in the playroom. "I was ready to have it out again. I love seeing your mama and Rosette with us. It's the only one we have of the whole family." Henry rested his arm around her shoulders.

"Oh, Daddy, missing them hurts so terribly." She laid her head on his shoulder.

"I know, dear. But what a blessing that your mama was able to meet Rosette. I'm sure they are loving each other so happily in heaven now. Maybe just waiting for the rest of us to catch up to them."

He turned and cupped her shoulders in his hands, looking intently into her eyes. "They wouldn't want us to cling to our grief. They know we miss them, but they would want us to do the best we can to live good lives without them, to bring joy to each other and to everyone we meet."

Jacquie nodded. She didn't want to agree, but she knew he was right.

She needed to let go of her pain. It wouldn't be a quick process, but she knew it was time to begin. She thought of Kevin. She certainly wasn't bringing him any joy.

"I shouldn't have left Kevin alone tonight. He's still recovering from the flu and that's miserable enough without feeling abandoned."

"Well then, let's eat quickly and send you home with some soup for him."

"And bread," she said. "It smells heavenly."

Driving home from her father's house, Jacquie took backroads that led her through a small forest that separated the city from the suburbs. It was a prettier drive than the highway and a few minutes shorter. On her right, a hillside rose above her. On her left, the hill dropped steeply, just beyond the far shoulder of the road. It was dusk, and a fog settled into the trees. Wisps of it eddied low across the pavement. As she rounded a curve, headlights were headed right for her!

She swerved right and pounded her full weight against the brake pedal, feeling her body strain back against the seat. A moment later she struck something, and as she lurched forward, her airbag exploded against her, throwing her back against the seat and stinging her face and chest. She expected to see the other car slammed against her own, but the deflated airbag revealed an empty road. She had collided with the guardrail on her right. Where had the other car gone?

Taking quick measure of herself, Jacquie was relieved to find she suffered no serious injuries. Her face felt burned, her shoulder and chest ached, but nothing worse. She checked in her side mirror, then opened her door. Illuminated by her car's dome light, dark tire marks told her the other car had skidded, then overcorrected, and disappeared through the opposite guardrail and down the hill. She grabbed her phone and, checking both ways, darted across.

A baby's cry reached her from far below. Her heart lurched as much for the frightened child as for her own lost daughter. She wanted to run away from her grief, from her loss, from this whole situation, but the insistence of the baby's screams wouldn't allow it. Edging down the steep hill she could barely make out the car that had skidded and rolled perhaps 100 feet, and now lay tipped, its front lifted by something near the bottom of the hill. Was she dreaming? Was she stuck in that recurring nightmare of the wreck she once witnessed?

She dialed a 9, but before she could press 11, she stumbled over a rock and tumbled forward. Sliding a good twenty feet before she could stop herself, the phone had flown out of her hand, and she could see no sign of it in the increasing darkness. She tried to stand, but her knee had twisted badly in her fall and wouldn't hold her weight. She looked down at the wreck below her and back up towards the road above her. The crying forced her decision. Someone had to comfort the baby; the driver must not be able to, and she was the only other person around. She gingerly slid on her bottom toward the car, following the path it had cleared.

Before she reached the wreck, she could see what looked like a log in otherwise flattened earth where the car had scraped the underbrush clear. Had the car rolled over the log, rather than bulldozing it out of its way? But when she neared it, she screamed in fright. A young woman had been thrown from the car and now lay looking at her with wide, unseeing eyes. The woman's arm lay extended toward her, and Jacquie scrambled back a few feet. Yet, the baby was still crying, and suddenly it seemed as if the woman reached out in a final supplication, pleading for someone to help the child. Jacquie eased around her, pulled herself up on her good leg, and was able to open the back door without making the car shift and fall. She unbuckled the screaming infant, who seemed about 3 months old. He was terrified, but the car seat had done its job and he was uninjured. Lifting him out, Jacquie gingerly settled back onto the ground, leaned against a tree, and rocked and held him against her chest until his crying quieted to whimpers and then snuffles. Amazingly, he fell asleep against her.

Then it was Jacquie's turn to cry, though her tears fell silently. She wept for the beauty of a sleeping child. She wept for the loss of her Rosette and her recent weeks of longing for this wonderful feeling of comforting a tiny one. And she wept for the woman, probably his mother, who died too young, and this child who would grow up not knowing her.

When her tears had run their course, Jacquie turned her thoughts to what faith she had left. Please, God, send someone to help us. There was no way she could safely climb the hill with her aching knee while holding a baby. Occasionally a car rumbled past on the road above her, but no one must have noticed the skids or broken guardrail. The damage to her car was on the side that wouldn't be seen as anyone drove past.

Please God, send someone to help us. Maybe Kevin would miss her and come looking for her. How long would she be down here holding this baby? When would the child wake and want to eat? She shivered. She wore her coat, and she zipped it around herself and the child, but the ground was damp, and the fog thickened with the darkness. Perhaps she should have stayed in the tilted car where they'd be more protected from the elements. No sooner had she thought that than it began to rain. She groaned.

The effort was awkward, but eventually with only one arm free and one good leg, she pulled herself to standing. She limp-hopped to the front of the car and saw that it was a boulder that had stopped the car's descent and had lifted the front half a couple feet off the ground. She nudged the car with her hip and found it to be fairly stable. Opening the backseat door again, she slid in and closed the door behind her quietly. The baby slept on. She looked at the car seat, knowing she could lay him in it and he would probably keep sleeping, but she continued to embrace him. She nuzzled the top of his head and inhaled the glorious aroma of a tiny human.

Thank you, God, for this opportunity. With a shock of guilt, she realized things could not have fared worse for the woman lying feet away, but they could have gone much worse for her and the child.

Thank you, God, that I didn't drink tonight. If her reaction speed had been at all affected by alcohol, she wouldn't be alive right now. She wouldn't have swerved as quickly and would have suffered a head-on collision. Thank you that I'm alive tonight. I may be cold and sore, but I'm alive, and so is this little angel.

She thought about Kevin. He loved her. He wanted to be with her. He'd have been devastated if she had died tonight, after losing their little Rosette. And her father, he'd lost his wife and then his only grandchild within weeks. Thank you, God, that he didn't lose his only daughter.

She looked out the window and could just make out the prone shape of the baby's mother, lifeless in the night. God, please comfort her family, whomever they are. Let me keep this child safe so he can be a help to them in their grief. Rosette had been a blessing to her when her mother died. The baby gave her a reason to keep living and a place to pour her love. Thank you, God, for Rosette. I wish I'd had her longer, but I thank you for the time that she was mine.

I mean ours.

Kevin loved Rosette as much as Jacquie did, she knew. And what had she done? Had she comforted him in his grief? No, she'd been too paralyzed by her own to reach out to him with anything but blame. Deep regret engulfed her. She had almost died without the chance to ask him to forgive her. She promised God she would the moment she saw him.

Jacquie looked up toward the road above her. Please, God, send someone to help us.

Night Shift

Immediately, there was a tapping on the window on the other side of the car seat. A woman peered in the window. Where in the world did she come from?

"Are you okay, Jacquie?" the woman asked.

Déjà vu! It was the same woman who had approached Jacquie's car once before. She had beamed like they were old friends and had said, "I'd recognize you anywhere. You look so much like your mother."

Jacquie closed her eyes in utter disbelief. "Miriam, right?" Wasn't everyone Miriam lately?

"Of course." Miriam opened the front seat side door and climbed in.

How did she do that? The front seat was a couple feet higher off the ground than the back seat, yet she hadn't seemed to struggle at all.

"My mother's friend?" Now Jacquie wondered if she had hit her head in the accident. Maybe she was hallucinating.

"How did you get here? Did you bring help?"

"Help will come, Jacquie. We have a while to wait. It is too late for Annette, bless her." She looked out toward the dark form. "But you and Sammy will be fine." She beamed a look of love at the child, and then at Jacquie. "In the meantime, I hear you've been wanting to interview me. What would you like to ask?"

Interview her? What a strange suggestion in the middle of the forest, sitting in a wrecked car with a dead woman only a few feet away. Jacquie rejected the idea, but seconds passed, and she sighed. Well, why not? All they could do was wait.

Where to begin? Jacquie wondered. "Who ARE you? Are you my dad's grocery lady? Are you the one who helped Gloria when her house was collapsing? Or are you one of lots of ladies who all call themselves Miriam and help people? And why, when I saw you last, did you say my mother sent her love?"

"That's a lot of questions. I'm not sure where to begin."

"Is there one of you, or many?"

Miriam chuckled. "There's only one of me, though I do get around. And thank you, by the way. Your 'Myriad Miriams' are doing wonderful things."

"My Myriad? It's the only possible explanation! Dozens of people wrote emails about Miriams who had helped them. But the descriptions were all different. Age, race, hair color, body build. The only thing in common was they all described someone very kind and cheerful. Are you a Master of Disguise? But why would you need disguises?"

"People must need me to look different. Perhaps I'm easier to relate to if I'm familiar in some way. Everyone looks alike inside, you know."

Totally confused, Jacquie shook her head. Her logical, skeptical mind resisted the possibility that there was something supernatural going on, but she couldn't come up with any other explanation, unless she really was hallucinating. "I suspect my father thinks you are Mary. You know, the Virgin Mary." She said it with a smile, assuming Miriam would laugh, or at least deny it.

Miriam nodded and smiled.

"No way!"

Miriam shrugged. "Your mother and my Son asked me to come and help you."

"Me? Not the other dozens of people who talk about how you came to their aid?"

"I came for you. Though I decided I might as well help some others, like Gloria, while I'm here. I have so many sons and daughters in need."

"Why me?"

"Why not? You are my daughter, too."

Baffled, or incredulous, Jacquie couldn't put her thoughts into words. Here she sat, presented with an unbelievable opportunity for a journalist, and she couldn't speak. Though who would believe her even if she told this tale in tomorrow's paper?

What should she ask? About the meaning of life? What heaven is like? Was Jesus really God? Did he know it as a kid? What was it like

157

mothering someone who was perfect?

After an uncomfortable silence, the soul-deep question that had burned in her heart and mind for weeks now escaped before she could stop it. "Why did Rosette die?"

At that moment the baby that Miriam called Sammy stirred and announced his hunger. Miriam lifted a diaper bag from the front seat floor to show her. From it, Miriam drew out a baby bottle of water and some powdered baby formula. Like an expert, she measured out the right amount of formula, poured it into the bottle and shook it. "I love the ingenuity that the Spirit leads people to tap and solve needs," she said. She also lifted a disposable diaper for Jacquie to see. "Not great for the environment, but certainly a blessing for harried parents these days. And here I thought washing machines were the ultimate convenience."

After Jacquie had changed Sammy and quieted him with the bottle, she drew her gaze from his dark eyes to let Miriam know she still waited for an answer.

Miriam nodded. "I know how deeply you hurt, how incapacitating the pain is that you feel. Jacquie, this life isn't the whole story. Rosette awaits you and lives now in indescribable joy. If you knew what she is experiencing, you wouldn't wish her back. You can be with her someday, and then for always. But yes, it is excruciating now. I remember when my Son died—"

Jacquie interrupted, "You only had three days to wait until He was with you again. If you are who you say you are." She didn't mean for her words to sound so accusatory, but anger lived right next door to her loss.

"You're right. We aren't in control of how long we wait until we reunite with our loved ones, but we can make the time a blessing to others. What you choose to do with your life will make a huge difference to others." She paused. "Kevin, for instance. And your father. They need your love. They are grieving, too."

Miriam looked at Jacquie with such compassion. Now she understood why so many people described their experience of this woman by mentioning her kind eyes.

"It wasn't Kevin's fault," Miriam murmured.

"No," Jacquie admitted.

"It wasn't yours either," Miriam said with authority.

Jacquie gasped, for the first time realizing that was her deepest fear.

Miriam nodded toward a now-sleeping Sammy. "See how gentle and loving you are with someone else's child? I know you were even more so with your own. And Rosette knows that, too. She overflows with love now, partially because of how much love she received from you and your whole family. Jacquie, it wasn't your fault."

Now Jacquie spoke through clenched teeth. "Then whose?"

"No, not our Heavenly Father's either. There is evil in this world. Sickness, disease, hatred, all the deadly sins for that matter, and horrible decisions." Miriam looked out toward the lifeless body. "Mistakes like texting while driving. But our Father can and does turn all the evil to good. And this life is not the end of the story. So much beauty and goodness and joy await."

"So why can't we skip this life and go right to the good stuff?"

"Relationship. Love."

"What?"

"You considered asking me about the meaning of life. Okay, here it is. This life is all about love and relationship. Loving God and others. Growing closer to God as you grow through your relationships. Love always involves sacrifice. It's like the proof that love is real. But it also always involves fruitfulness. Love grows. It creates. It blooms into something new. Learning through love is what this life on earth is all about. God is so amazingly good!" Miriam's face glowed with her adoration. "We love and sacrifice. That love blooms and creates, all the while building beautiful relationships that exist in the image and likeness of God. God is the perfectly loving relationship between Father, Son, and Spirit."

Jacquie pondered this, not fully understanding it, but acknowledging deep in her soul that Miriam spoke profound truth. Her love for her parents, Kevin, and especially Rosette felt like it participated in the divine. "Love never ends," she whispered.

"Exactly," Miriam answered.

"I loved Rosette. I loved my mother. That love continues even now that they are gone." She wasn't sure she was grasping it all, but she suddenly, intensely knew her mother and Rosette were still in existence, somewhere, some way.

Miriam nodded. "You will be with them in the fullness of time, and they are with you now."

The thought brought deep comfort, the first true comfort Jacquie had felt since Rosette died.

After a quiet time, Jacquie looked out the window. "When help comes, you'll be gone, won't you?"

"I'll always be nearby, but you are right, I won't be seen."

"I wish I had let you stay in my car the first time you tried. We could have had so much more time together."

"You weren't ready yet."

"No, I guess I wasn't. I'm not sure if I'm ready now. And if I am, what am I ready for?"

Sammy stirred in his sleep, and love washed over Jacquie. Yes, she would need to relinquish this child to his family before long, but she loved him now and it was worth it, no matter what lay ahead. Rosette had been worth it, no matter how short their lives together. Another baby would never replace Rosette, but she would love that child every bit as much, even knowing all parents eventually have to let go.

CHAPTER 20

Kevin startled awake on the couch in the small hours of the morning and realized Jacquie hadn't roused him when she got home from visiting her father. He dragged himself upstairs, still half asleep, but came fully awake when he saw their bed empty. She hadn't come home from her father's house at all. Remembering his mother's tendency, not long before she left, to be gone all night on a drinking binge brought back all the emotions of a frightened ten-year-old.

Where was Jacquie? Overindulging at a bar? Sleeping off the effects afterwards somewhere? No, he tried to tell himself, Jacquie wouldn't do that. She promised she wouldn't drink anymore.

But he remembered the anger and hopelessness he had felt when he'd come home and found Jacquie's empty liquor bottles on the porch. Hadn't he heard his mother promise the same thing to his father? To him? Over and over.

He realized he was pacing. He sat to try to think of what he should do. "Pack and leave," he grumbled.

Then Yosef's face came to mind along with his words, "It sounds like your wife needs protecting now."

Where did that come from? Kevin took a deep breath, trying to calm himself. He could call her!

He dialed her number and only heard it ring and ring. Where could she be?

More of Yosef's words came to Kevin. "She's broken hearted. She needs you, and she's worth it."

He could call Henry, to see if she really had gone to visit him. He could ask when she left. But what good would it do to wake his father-in-law? He'd simply be sharing his worry and doubts. Henry didn't need that.

Maybe she was tired and decided to spend the night with her dad, rather than drive home. "She would have called me," he answered himself.

Then Kevin's tired mind led him through one devastating scenario after another. She has been so depressed. Would she have been sad enough to try to harm herself? She might be at a hospital!

Or she might have left him! She might be driving farther and farther away from him right now.

He dressed, and grabbed his jacket, wallet, and keys, determined not to let her leave him like his mother had. Dawn lightened the sky by the time he had searched for her car around nearby bars, and he decided to drive Jacquie's usual route to his father-in-law's house. As he came around a curve, he saw three things almost simultaneously: Jacquie's car on the side of the road, skid marks crossing the lanes near it, and a demolished guard rail.

His stomach lurched as he braked hard and parked behind his wife's car. He ran to its passenger side, away from possible traffic, and found it empty and badly damaged. He dropped to his knees. Dear God! Please let Jacquie be all right. Help me find her. I swear I'll be the best man, the best husband, and if You're willing, the best father I can possibly be.

Frightened, but determined, he crossed the road and peered down the hillside. It was obvious a car had careened off the road. Skid marks in the pine needles continued for about 50 feet, and then foliage lay broken or crushed in a swath as far downhill as he could see.

"Jacquie! Jacquie! Where are you? Are you down there?"

When he heard no answer, he ran back to his car and honked the horn, then listened for her call, her voice, anything that would tell him she was alive. He heard an answering horn from below him!

He patted his pocket reassuring himself he had his phone, then began to climb carefully down the hill. The honking repeated, assuring him he was headed in the right direction to someone. He tried to figure out what had happened. Jacquie must have seen the other car go off. Maybe she headed down to help. But then why didn't she phone for help? He looked at his phone. It had reception. He hadn't taken time to look in her car. Maybe she left her phone there.

Once again, the honking repeated and he wished he could move faster, but the light was still not strong enough to show him what lay below him, or even the safest path beyond a few yards ahead.

Then he heard a baby cry. He was close enough for voices to carry.

"Jacquie!" he called.

"Kevin!" he heard. Her voice was muffled, but it was definitely his wife!

Finally, he could see a car at rest, its front tilted up at an angle, and beside it, a woman's body. He didn't check for a pulse when he made his way to her. The open eyes and white face told him he couldn't help her. What condition would his wife be in?

He peered in the window of the car, and relief, or the rapid climb down, made his legs begin to shake. Inside the backseat next to an infant car seat, his wife sat calming a baby. She looked exhausted, but she smiled at him and her smile filled him with such a mixture of emotions that he wouldn't have names for all his feelings.

"Are you okay?" he managed to ask.

"We both are," she answered, still grinning. "Well, my knee is wonky. I couldn't make it up the hill carrying Sammy. Kevin, I'm sorry for how I've treated you."

Kevin shrugged, then made it around the car to the other side, opened the door, and reached for the baby, who smiled up at him and patted his cheek, which destroyed the last bit of self-control Kevin had managed. He burst into sobs and had to sit down on the ground, carefully pulling the baby close to his chest.

Jacquie eased herself out of the car, favoring her right knee, and as if it explained everything said, "Miriam was here."

He hoped Miriam wasn't the woman lying dead a few feet away. And he hoped his wife wasn't suffering from a concussion and losing touch with reality, because no one else was near.

Whatever the case, he shifted the baby and drew his phone from his pocket, dialing 911 with his thumb.

CHAPTER 21

Jacquie awoke in the hospital feeling groggy from anesthesia after knee surgery.

Paramedics had arrived shortly after Kevin called them and hoisted her back up to the roadside. They were lifting her into an ambulance when she watched them bring up the now-wrapped body of Sammy's mother. But the most difficult part of the whole experience was giving Sammy up to the police. The paramedics complimented her on her care for the sweet baby, deciding she and the car seat had done so well that he probably wouldn't need more than a quick check at the hospital. They would try to contact the baby's family and promised they would report back to her when they delivered him to loving arms.

"I'll take him," she had told them. "I'll take him if he doesn't have anyone else."

Now Kevin walked alongside, holding her hand, as they rolled her bed out of recovery. He had stayed with her until they took her away for surgery and had waited while she was in the recovery area. Now wheeled into a regular room, she discovered her father waited for her. "I'm okay, Daddy, she reassured him. Just a banged-up knee."

"Thank God," Henry said. He nodded hello to Kevin. "You've taken good care of our girl."

"Scared me when I realized she hadn't made it home last night," Kevin said.

"I wondered how long it would take before you missed me," Jacquie said, but smiled to let him know she was just happy to have been found. "Have you heard any more about Sammy?"

A nurse had just entered. "Is that the little baby you rescued? Sounds like you were quite the hero last night." She took Jacquie's vitals.

"I just did what needed to be done. Did they find his family?"

"I'll go see what I can find out. You try not to get worked up, though, you hear?"

"That's my girl," said Henry. "A heroine."

She smiled lopsided at him. "Aw, Dad. It wasn't just me. I climbed down and helped him stop crying, but it was Miriam who found the diaper bag so I could feed him.

"Miriam?" her father asked, one eyebrow raised. "So, you finally met my Miriam?"

"I did," she said. "And I'm a believer." She stayed with me until we heard Kevin calling for me. What an amazing... woman!"

She then looked meaningfully at Kevin. "It felt good to have a baby in my arms again."

"Me, too," he said, and squeezed her hand.

Hours later, a woman with greying hair and a grandma-smile came into Jacquie's hospital room, carrying a very sleepy baby.

"Sammy!" Jacquie whispered. "I've missed you." She turned to the woman, "Is he okay? I'm so sorry about his mama."

"How did you know his name?" the woman asked, but then shrugged. "I came to thank you. My son is taking it pretty hard, but it would have been so much worse if Sammy hadn't made it. If you hadn't gone down to him, no telling how long it would have been before someone would have found him and could calm him and hold him and feed him." The woman caught a sob that tried to escape. "I just wanted to thank you personally."

Regaining her control, she continued with compassion in her voice. "I heard from the nurses that you lost your little one at about Sammy's age. We'll leave our phone number. You can call anytime if you'd like to visit."

Now it was Jacquie's turn to fight back tears. "Holding him all night was a blessing. I think he has helped me start to heal."

Jacquie's next visitor was Gloria, who slipped in while Kevin and Henry were having lunch in the cafeteria.

"Well this is different, having you come to me," said Jacquie.

"How are you feeling? You must have been terrified."

"Strangely, I wasn't. First, I was determined to help a baby stop crying. Next, I was caught up in the wonder of holding a baby again." She lowered her voice. "Then, I finally found—or I should say—your Miriam found me."

"Ooo, isn't she wonderful? Tell me all about it!"

Jacquie recounted her night with Miriam, and Gloria listened intently.

"So, do you think she really is...?" asked Gloria.

"I do! I can't believe it myself, but I do. I keep asking, why would she come to see me? Why would God send her to me?"

"I think I finally have come to that realization, too, as well as the same question, why me?"

"Judging from all the people who wrote to me after my article, I don't think it was just us. I think she came and helped lots of people, but you and my dad and I are the only ones she visited repeatedly."

Gloria laughed. "Maybe we're slow learners! Or maybe we should simply accept that God loves us!" Then she offered Jacquie a small gift bag. "This is actually from Miriam. She visited me early yesterday morning to say goodbye and asked me to give this to you when I saw you at the hospital, for your next baby. I thought she meant I should visit you when your next baby is born. But then to hear you were in the hospital now, I think she meant for you to save it for your next baby."

"My next baby?" Miriam must know something I don't know. Jacquie opened the bag. "What a beautiful little lamb!"

"Isn't it? She said her husband Yosef carved it from olive wood from her homeland."

"So... Yosef, as in Joseph?"

"I assume so."

"You know, my husband Kevin met Yosef a couple of times, here in a diner. He mentioned returning from the desert."

"Possibly the same desert where he led my husband to safety on a donkey, which, by the way, he carved for Daniel and Winnie."

"Amazing," was all Jacquie could say.

And Gloria could only nod.

One Last Night Shift

Miriam walked in the dark along paths edged with budding rhododendrons, azaleas, and unspiraling ferns, beneath giant evergreens. She remembered warmly a little boy who had asked her to intercede for his mother as she lay near death after the birth of his tiny sister. Both mother and child had lived, and years later the boy, by then Father Ambrose Mayer, had built this Portland place of peace and refuge, the National Sanctuary of Our Sorrowful Mother, as a sign of his gratitude. Arriving at a stone grotto carved into a 100-foot basalt cliffside, she settled onto a kneeler before a white statue replica of Michelangelo's Pietà that depicted Mary holding the body of her Son after His crucifixion.

Her thoughts focused on the statue and beyond it to her experience of that devastating moment. She ached anew with the anguish of holding her Son's lifeless adult body upon her lap. But the pain didn't stand alone, for alongside it was boundless gratitude for the sacrifice her Son had made to redeem all her children.

His was no quick death. He had suffered intensely on that final day: whipping, beating, humiliation, a piercing thorny crown shoved down upon his brow, dragging a heavy beam—not to be honed into something sturdy and functional like He and Joseph had built—but wood of torture and death, and then, oh then—she still could hear the terrible blows—the pounding of spikes to peg His hands and feet to the cross, His groans as the cross was lifted and dropped into its hole, the draining of His strength over three hours while she stayed within His gaze, before His forgiving words, His release of His Spirit, and the final thrust of a spear that confirmed He was dead.

She could feel the tears trailing her cheeks as they had countless times when she commemorated His suffering and death. She remembered following His footsteps on the Way of the Cross, or the Via Dolorosa, in order to ponder the mysteries of His death. She wept for the wounds people today continue to inflict on her Son: the commandments they break, their refusal to center their lives around the One who loves them, their selfishness that hurts the ones around them. She cried for the pain her beloved children experienced at the hands of her other, also-beloved children.

Yet, she forced herself to remember His resurrection! For as surely as He had died, He had also risen.

The dawning sun brightened the sky above the Grotto and drew her gaze heavenward. His resurrection was the culmination of those three agonizing days when her Son was lost to her.

He rose and returned to her!

At this thought, her soul leapt within her and her joy resurged. For as deep as her sorrow had been—and still was when she pondered His suffering—her joy was even greater. He lived! He had conquered not only death, but sin and evil. That was the purpose behind His suffering, and what a joyous gift it was to all who welcomed it, who welcomed Him into their hearts. The thought reminded Miriam of her countless children who do strive to follow God's path.

Exultation encompassed Miriam, and she lifted her love to her God and thanked Him with her whole being. God—Father, Son, and Spirit—God was infinitely good. God was all Love, and she was entirely His. All her children were God's, and she would work tirelessly for them to realize that, so they could share in her Joy.

A young priest passed behind Miriam on his way to celebrate the first Mass of the day. He had been struggling with depression and loneliness and had knelt a few feet behind the praying woman to ask God to give him strength.

He watched Miriam raise her arms and listened while she sang with great elation:

My soul magnifies the Lord and my spirit rejoices in God, my Savior…
for He has looked with favor on His humble servant.
From this day all generations will call me blessed,
the Almighty has done great things for me,
and holy is His Name.
He has mercy on those who fear Him
in every generation.
He has shown the strength of His arm,
He has scattered the proud in their conceit.
He has cast down the mighty from their thrones,

and has lifted up the humble.
He has filled the hungry with good things,
and the rich He has sent away empty.
He has come to the help of his servant Israel
for He has remembered his promise of mercy,
the promise He made to our fathers,
to Abraham and his children forever.
Glory to the Father, and to the Son, and to the Holy Spirit,
as it was in the beginning, is now, and will be forever.
Amen. Alleluia!

The sun crested the grotto edge, temporarily blinding the young priest. When he shaded his eyes with his hand, the woman was gone.

Yet, such ecstasy had risen in him as he overheard her words that simply recalling the experience overcame any emergence of darkness in his mood for all his remaining years of life.

The End

ABOUT THE AUTHOR

Betty Arrigotti lives near Portland, Oregon with her husband George and her mother Ruth. With four daughters and eight grandchildren, family ranks high on her priority list, above crocheting, gardening, reading, and yes, even writing.

Please visit her website at BettyArrigotti.com to learn more about her non-fiction writing, including reviews of self-help and spirituality books on topics such as relationships, fear, joy, finances, or mercy.

She loves to hear from readers! Please email her: Betty@Arrigotti.com

ALSO FROM THE AUTHOR:

Betty has written four Contemporary Christian Romances and uses both her spiritual and counseling education to bring depth to her novels.

- *Hope and a Future* offers marriage counseling insights as the romances unfold.
- The sequel, **Where Hope Leads**, takes place in Ireland and does the same with pre-marriage counseling.
- **When the Vow Breaks** portrays the damage that family secrets can wreak on the innocent, though grace can heal them.
- *Their Only Hope* takes a darker turn and enters the world of human trafficking as a young man helps a young woman escape.

Made in the USA
Lexington, KY
20 November 2019